THE MONSTERS OF CHAVEZ RAVINE

DEBRA CASTANEDA

HAPPY
Birthday!
Dearest Drake ♡
YVOD
(>.<:)
2021

SECOND
RODEO
— BOOKS —

ISBN: 978-1-7353420-1-6
Cover design by: James, GoOnWrite.com
Map Illustration by: Dewi Hargreaves

To my family, who once called Palo Verde home.

Table of Contents

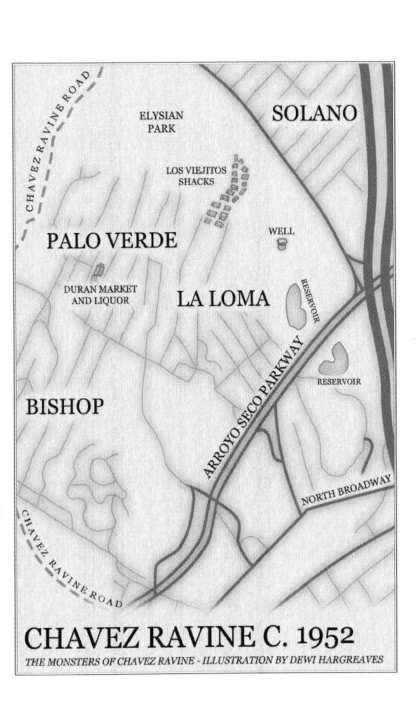

CHAVEZ RAVINE C. 1952

THE MONSTERS OF CHAVEZ RAVINE - ILLUSTRATION BY DEWI HARGREAVES

Chapter 1

Los Angeles, Autumn 1952

Her father's messengers arrived one by one throughout the morning, leaving Trini Duran to conclude she had wasted her time nagging him to get a telephone. He didn't need one. Not when he had his friends to do his bidding.

By ten o'clock, she'd heard, "Ai, Trini, it's so sad your father is up there all alone."

By eleven, "If you want my honest opinion, Trini, he's not looking so good these days."

And by the time lunch rolled around, a comment so sharp it could have poked her in the eye. "God have mercy on your soul, Trini, for abandoning your father like you did."

When Trini overheard her boss talking on the phone, she escaped to the shed outside the back of the store where she could eat her lunch in peace. She sat down on a rickety chair and swatted away a fly. A bee appeared through a crack in the wooden slats, buzzing near her sandwich. Several ants crawled up her socked foot. She had dispatched the pests when the door flew open. Henry Loya stood there, regarding her solemnly.

"Your father says you need to go home," he said without preamble. Just one of the reasons Trini liked the man. He didn't beat around the bush.

She rose with a sigh. "Now what?"

Henry hesitated, looking troubled. "He said some weird stuff is going on, but he wouldn't say what. Said he needed to show you in person."

"What kind of stuff?" she asked, feeling a knot in her belly.

With her father, if it wasn't one thing, it was another. A new customer he thought was a spy from the California Housing Authority. Another visit from a city official threatening to kick him out of Chavez Ravine, once and for all.

It was Henry's turn to sigh. "You know how your father is. He wouldn't tell me." He paused. "Look, Trini. I've tried talking to him. Told him he didn't have to stay. That he could take the money, close up. Retire, or open a new market in the empty store in Lincoln Heights."

By this time, Trini had lost her appetite. She stuffed what remained of the sandwich in her apron pocket. "That's what I keep telling him, but he won't listen."

Henry gave an indulgent smile. "He's as stubborn as the rest of them. But, Trini, I think you should go. Something's not right. I can feel it."

Trini stared at him in surprise. She'd worked for Henry Loya for one year, and during that time, he'd never said a word about leaving her father behind. Which made him the only person she knew who hadn't tried to make her feel guilty. Not that she needed any help in that department. She felt lousy about it every single day.

"Okay, I'll go," she lied.

She didn't like to go against Henry, especially not after everything he'd done for her, giving her a job and a place to live. Making it possible for her to take classes at L.A. City College, which reminded her—she needed to study. Her father and his Chavez Ravine problems would have to wait. Besides, she and her brother had begged him to sell his properties to the city. Beto had even invited him to Pico Rivera, where he and his family had moved.

Salvio Duran would not budge. He'd been born in the Palo Verde neighborhood of Chavez Ravine, and he would die there, he announced to anyone who would listen, and to hell with the city and their stupid plan to build low-income housing.

"But it's eminent domain, viejo," Ripper had pleaded. "You don't have any choice. Nobody does."

Even former convicts like Ripper Cuevas knew about "eminent domain." Ripper managed Henry's second market in Boyle Heights. Trini liked him, even if some of the old people still held it against him that he did time in prison. But Ripper was a hard worker and didn't talk much, and he'd tried to convince her father it was useless to continue fighting against the city and its pinche plan to build cheap apartments for people who already had houses with yards.

Trini followed Henry back into the market, suddenly busy with women shopping for dinner. She took her place at the cash register. Of all the jobs she did at Loya Market, this was her favorite, even though she sometimes had to talk to the customers—it beat stocking the shelves or cleaning out the refrigerators, but she thought all that yakking was annoying. Which explained why the customers preferred talking to Henry. Often, they did more talking than buying, but Henry didn't seem to mind.

Late in the afternoon—another warm fall day in Los Angeles—a small group had gathered on the benches outside the entrance. She peered outside. By their angry faces and all the hand waving, she could guess what they were talking about—Chavez Ravine. No matter how hard she tried, she couldn't seem to escape the place.

3

She recognized Rose and Martin, friends of her father, and somebody new joined them. It couldn't be.

Yes, it was. Bobby Guerra.

What the hell was he doing here? She'd grown up with him in Palo Verde. He was a couple of years ahead of her in school. He'd disappeared for a while and later, she heard he'd gone to college. A few months ago, he turned up again, working as a community organizer. Precisely what that meant, Trini had no idea, but she was sure it involved talking people into stuff because the guy had always been a smooth talker.

She scurried to the bathroom and checked her hair. It was shiny and clean, at least. Good thing she'd washed it the night before. She dug out a tube of lipstick. A swipe of red did the trick, and just in time, too. She had resumed her place at the cash register, determined to ignore him when Bobby walked in. He grabbed a bunch of Cokes and set them down in front of her.

"You drinking all those?" she asked.

"Nice to see you, too, Trini," he said, lifting a single eyebrow.

She rang him up and held out her hand. He slapped a dollar into her palm, never taking his eyes off her face. "Has anyone ever told you it's rude to stare?" she snapped.

Bobby grinned. "Is this how you treat your customers?"

"Only the ones who get on my nerves," she replied, handing him his change.

"I can see you haven't changed a bit, Trini," Bobby said over his shoulder, smiling as he strode toward the door.

She watched as he handed out Cokes to the small group outside. Her heart was beating so hard she had to sit down for a few seconds to calm down. He'd become even better looking with those white teeth, smooth brown skin and strong jaw of his. Bits and pieces of their conversation drifted through the screen door—substandard housing, fair market value, holdouts.

4

When she wandered over to the window, pretending to straighten up the "Today's Sale" sign, he was still out there, talking. He caught her looking and waved for her to join them.

"No, thank you," she mouthed, shaking her head. After learning her lesson the hard way, she'd rather stick a needle in her eye. All those city people who made decisions about Chavez Ravine were nothing but liars and tricksters, and no amount of meetings or protest signs would change things.

She picked up a duster and began swiping at the shelves, her back turned to the plate glass window. Didn't Bobby have more important things to do than hang around the market?

Henry walked back in, went to his tiny office at the back of the market, and returned, jacket in hand. He sighed. "Can you close up, Trini? Bobby's talked me into going to one of those damned city meetings. Wants me to give a speech." Trini blinked in surprise. Henry rarely cursed.

"Isn't it too late?" she asked. "I thought the city already decided."

Henry shrugged. "That's what I keep telling him, but he's like your father. Stubborn as they come. And speaking of your father, you said you'd go see him. Don't forget."

"I won't," she said, crossing her fingers behind her back.

The last thing she wanted to do was go all the way to Chavez Ravine and get an earful from her father. She'd see him in a few days and give him a chance to calm down. Bring him an apple pie and cook his favorite dinner when she got there, even get her good-for-nothing brother Beto to do his part and visit the man if he could drag himself away from Pico Rivera. In the meantime, she had plenty to keep her busy. Besides all the studying she needed to do, there was that new book she'd checked out from the library and the movie at the Vern Theater she'd meant to see. Tomorrow was her day off, and she deserved a treat. Already feeling better about things, Trini managed a smile at Rose when she ducked in to say hello. Bobby came in, too.

"I'll see you around, Trini," he said, looking her over again in that way of his.

"If you say so, Mister Community Organizer," she said, turning around and walking toward the back of the store.

Her face felt like it was on fire. When she looked over her shoulder, Bobby was still standing there, smirking. Then he winked, turned on his heel, and left.

Chapter 2

Trini sat in the morning sun, enjoying a cigarette and a cup of coffee, her reward for rising early and getting all the wash done, even the sheets.

The laundry flapped in the slight breeze, blocking her view of the Loya's freshly painted white clapboard house. Not that she needed the extra privacy. Henry's wife, Esther, had plenty to keep her busy without sticking her nose in Trini's business, and she wasn't a big talker, either—another point in her favor.

In fact, Trini couldn't believe her luck. The tiny cottage at the back of the Loya property suited her perfectly. It was a bedroom, bathroom, kitchen, and a skinny sunroom that ran the cottage's length, and the rent was dirt cheap. All she had to do was help the Loya boys with their homework—they were terrible at math—and run errands for Esther, who never learned to drive and refused to take the bus.

At first, she'd been nervous about living so close to her boss and his family, but it had worked out better than she hoped, and she rarely heard them talk about Chavez Ravine. What was done was done; this was their attitude.

Unlike her father, Henry was a practical man, and as soon as he realized the city would eventually force everyone out, he sold up.

It had been a relief to move down into the city and escape the constant nagging she'd faced when she lived with her father. "Ai, Trini, you should get married. You're twenty-two. Settle down. Have some kids. You should put those books down and start looking for a man."

The rest of the morning, she spent cleaning the cottage, throwing open the windows of the sunroom to air out the place, scrubbing the clawfoot bathtub, mopping the red linoleum floor, and even sweeping under the bed.

For lunch, she heated a can of Campbell's tomato soup and made a quesadilla, reading "Rebecca" while she ate. Instead of studying, like she'd intended, she took her book into the sunroom and continued to read, stretched out on a cot she'd bought second-hand for overnight guests—not that she'd had any. She'd meant to invite her old friend Weechie, stuck in Bishop with her family, but she hadn't gotten around to it because Weechie sometimes got on her nerves. If she came, she'd start talking about tough times in Chavez Ravine, and there would be no shutting her up.

She must have dozed off because the next thing she knew, someone was banging on her door. Probably the Loya boys, the one drawback to her living situation. They had no respect for her days off. Well, they could wait a few seconds until she went to the bathroom. The banging continued.

When she opened the door a crack and peered out, her heart sank.

There stood Bertita and Lencha—worse than the Loya boys. Much worse. They'd been her mother's closest friends, and by the look on their determined faces, it would not be easy to get rid of them.

Bertita used her cane to push open the door. "Are you going to keep us standing out here forever?" she demanded.

8

"Ai, no. Come in, come in," she said, pulling them inside. The ladies hardly ever ventured outside Chavez Ravine, which meant whatever brought them to her door was serious.

Lencha handed her a paper bag filled with Mexican sweet bread. Trini made a fresh pot of coffee and set the table as the two women wandered around and inspected the cottage with open curiosity. She kept a close eye on Lencha—the woman was a curandera who dabbled in witchcraft, at least that's what her mother used to say. Trini wouldn't put it past her to slip something under her bed, something with a spell to make her go back home.

Bertita sat down with a grunt and dipped a semita into her coffee. "This place is nice," she said, sounding surprised. "Real cute," she added a moment later.

Lencha nudged Bertita, who shot her a stern look. "Let the girl have her concha." Lencha shrugged and helped herself to an elote.

Trini nibbled her sweet bread and braced herself. The ladies were not their usual perky selves, which meant something was going on, but she was determined not to ask. Lencha's mouth stretched into a grim line. Bertita had dark shadows under her deep-set eyes, and her long face had taken on a skeletal appearance. A brimmed cap sat at a jaunty angle on her head, but the colorful scarf she wore wrapped around her hair did little to brighten her pale skin. No use asking if she'd like to take it off. Trini had never seen her without it. Lencha had polished off her elote and was brushing crumbs off her lap, frowning.

Trini watched both women warily. It was hard to tell who would strike first.

Bertita grabbed her cane and thumped the floor with it. Trini jumped.

"When was the last time you came home?" Bertita asked.

Trini crossed her arms in front of her chest. "I don't live there anymore," she replied, congratulating herself on her answer.

Bertita and Lencha exchanged looks. "I told you she was going to be like this," Lencha said with a heavy sigh.

"I'm not being like anything," Trini protested. "I moved out a year ago."

"You know what I meant," said Bertita. "I *meant* when was the last time you visited your father?"

Trini avoided their stares by topping off their coffee. It also gave her time to think. She couldn't remember. Had an entire month gone by since she'd convinced her father to meet her at Philippe's in downtown for lunch?

She shrugged. "Not that long ago."

"Mentirosa," Bertita muttered. Great, now they were calling her a liar.

Lencha nudged Bertita. "Go on, tell her."

Trini glanced longingly at her copy of "Rebecca" sitting on a shelf. There was no telling how long the visit was going to last. "Tell me what?"

Bertita shook her head as she nudged Lencha. "She won't believe us."

Trini stood up and began collecting dishes from the table. "Whatever it is, please say it."

Bertita hesitated. Finally, she adjusted her cap and said, "It's a long story, and we have to get back, but we think somebody is up to no good, playing tricks on your father. It's got him all upset. Lencha makes him a special drink to calm his nerves, but he's all worked up, and he keeps asking for you."

At this, Trini felt a twinge of unease. "What kind of tricks?"

Bertita stood up. She was a tall woman. Taller even than most men. "The bad kind," she said. "The kind that gives old people heart attacks and kills them."

Trini flinched, feeling a sudden coldness sweep through her. Bertita was on dangerous ground, and, by the looks on their faces, they knew it. Her mother, Petra, had died of a massive stroke two days after the family received the Housing Authority's eviction letter in the summer of 1950. Everyone blamed the devastating bombshell for her death—the shock, they said, was too much for her.

Trini had stayed in Chavez Ravine for a year, comforting her father as best she could and running the store, but the longer she remained, the angrier she'd become, furious with all the uppity city officials and the people tricked into believing the city would ever listen to them. Her father had begged her not to leave, but she couldn't take it anymore. She had to get on with her life. Staying in Chavez Ravine would have meant agreeing to live in limbo.

Trini glanced at Lencha, who was shaking her head. Whatever was going on, the two ladies didn't seem in agreement.

Lencha surprised her by grabbing both her hands and giving them a shake. "Listen, Trini, now's not the time to be stubborn. No one's asking you to move home. All we want is for you to go see your father. That's all. You can come back with us ahora."

"I might have to close the market for Henry," she lied, walking them to the door.

When they'd finally said their goodbyes, making one last plea for her to visit, they left.

Trini grabbed her book and flopped on the cot in the sunroom. Determined to make the most of her day off, she planned on reading for the rest of the afternoon. She had an early shift at the store the next day. There would be plenty of time for a visit after work.

Chapter 3

It was a long business getting to Chavez Ravine. Trini took the number ten streetcar, then walked Bishop Road under the Arroyo Secco Parkway and made her way up a dirt path into the neighborhood of La Loma, one of three that made up Chavez Ravine.

The trail was dry and cracked beneath her feet, tall yellow grass waving lazily in the slight breeze. She stopped several times to pick foxtails from her socks. The bustling streets of Los Angeles seemed far away. She turned and watched a few cars drive by on Solano Avenue. The Navarro family, she heard, had taken an offer from the city and bought a house down there, smaller and more expensive than the one they'd owned on Pine Street. They wanted to stay as close to La Loma as possible so they could hear the coyotes at night.

She passed the Post Office, closed, and so was the shop that sold American foods. She made a mental note to tell her father he needed to order that stuff. Despite what he thought, customers wanted more than flour, rice, and beans.

The familiar streets had mostly emptied—Agua Pura Drive, Brooks Avenue, Yolo Drive—but she spotted some signs of life here and there. A neatly tended yard, a car parked in front of a house, a goat tethered on a steep hillside. The children, though, she'd not seen one. The place had gone downhill in the short time since she last visited, with weeds growing everywhere, and fences falling.

Chavez Ravine was becoming a ghost town, and if she was honest, it gave her the creeps.

After a couple more blocks, she didn't think she could stand looking at another abandoned house or rusted, broken-down jalopy.

Before the city had come up with its dumb plan to build low-income housing and had sent all those insulting eviction letters, Chavez Ravine was a lively place. Since then, most of the people had sold up and left.

How could her father and the last remaining holdouts stand living in a place half dead? It was downright depressing and lonely.

She passed Vera Salcedo on Effie Street, sitting on the porch of her sad specimen of a house. The place looked more ramshackle than ever.

Vera shook a fist and shouted, "Traitor!"

Trini paused by the front gate. "You need anything from the store, Vera?" But the old lady wasn't interested in anything besides hurling more insults, so Trini moved on, vowing to avoid the street again.

Getting off the road was a good idea. There was no telling who else she might run into. Everyone in Chavez Ravine knew everybody's business, including hers, and there was no shortage of people who would tell her to her face what they thought of her leaving her father.

She ducked into a skinny dirt path that led to Palo Verde. It would take longer to get there, but it was a pretty walk, even though it involved walking up a slope. As soon as she entered the shade of the wood, she felt an odd reluctance to go any further and stood, contemplating turning around. Some trees were dead and rotting. A small animal skittered over dried leaves, making her

14

jump as it ran past, its tail weirdly malformed. She looked around nervously, then scolded herself for being such a scaredy-cat.

Taking a deep breath, she hurriedly crossed the uneven ground, her hair catching in a tree branch. She freed herself and seconds later snagged her sweater on a shrub. Cursing, she smoothed down her hair, then set out again. She had not gone far when a root tripped her up, sending her stumbling, pitching forward into the dirt.

Swearing again, she rolled to her feet and took stock. She'd scraped her hands, and a painful lump had begun to form on her right knee. Gritting her teeth, she started walking again.

A few yards later, she stopped, disoriented.

Was Palo Verde straight ahead or somewhere off to the left? She used to know every bit of wood, hill, and gully in the area. Her mother used to threaten her with the Cucuy to keep her from wandering too far from the house, but not even that had stopped her from exploring.

After all these months, she must have lost her sense of direction. She looked around, jaw tightening, hands clenched. The wood was thicker and darker than she remembered, forming a canopy that sucked out the light. And where were the birds? There was not a chirp or tweet in the branches overhead, which were lower than she recalled.

Still, it wasn't like she was in the middle of nowhere. She wasn't lost. She could spin around and walk east or west, and she'd end up somewhere familiar. So why was her heart beating so fast?

A noise behind her made her eyes snap open, and she turned around.

Someone stood there in the gloom under a tree. Dressed head to toe in white, with a head covering. Like a long, lacy wedding veil, but tattered. She could not make out the face. She stared in confusion. It was as still as a statue.

"Hello?" she called, then waited, heart pounding.

Seconds went by—an eternity. "Hey," Trini finally said, "What's your name? Are you lost or something?" She wished her voice didn't sound so shaky.

No answer came. A slight breeze rustled through the tops of the trees.

Trini waved her hands over her head and stomped her feet, but the figure in white did not react. It remained motionless, radiating a vague menace, filling her with unease that was fast turning to fear. She glanced around for something she could use as a weapon and picked up a rock, hoping she was overreacting and would not need to throw it.

A flurry of air swept through the clearing, lifting the veil on the mysterious figure, revealing the face of a long-snouted dog with glittering black eyes.

Trini gasped.

Either someone was playing a trick, or all the silly talk about weird things happening in Chavez Ravine had got to her. A joke, she decided—a mean one. The idiot was probably wearing a mask. A good one, she had to admit. Well, there was one way to deal with that.

She threw the rock as hard as she could. Then she ran.

Chapter 4

Trini limped into Duran Market & Liquor, determined to keep her mouth shut. If she told anyone about the freak who tried to scare her in the woods between Loma and Palo Verde, she'd hear, "I told you so" until the day she died.

Her father's face wore a strained look. Salvio Duran sat on a stool behind the cash register. He jumped when she banged through the door. Her eyes narrowed as he reached instinctively under the counter. The man insisted on keeping a gun around in case thugs tried to hold him up.

"You plan on shooting your own daughter?" she asked.

Salvio crossed his arms in front of his chest and scowled. "I still have a daughter? That's news to me."

Trini crossed the room, leaned over the counter, and kissed his forehead. Then she surveyed the store with a critical eye. The wooden floor needed a good mopping. A fine layer of dust covered the shelves. Canned food sat in unopened boxes. There wasn't a fresh vegetable or fruit in sight, but there were plenty of the usual staples: bags of rice, beans, flour, and sugar. She went over to the refrigerator and peered through the glass. The milk looked good. Plenty of cold beer and wine. At least her father hadn't completely lost his mind. Liquor sales made up more than half the market's business.

The place had gone downhill since she had left. She sighed, turning her attention to her father, who watched her every move with troubled eyes. His thick salt and pepper hair—his one vanity—had lost its luster. His muscles had also vanished, so he appeared shrunken in his clothes. He didn't look good. Trini felt a prickle of worry.

"I heard you haven't been feeling so great," she began cautiously. They'd entered tricky territory. She needed to figure out what exactly was wrong without getting dragged into another scheme to get her to move back home.

He shrugged. "It's impossible to sleep around here." He paused. "These days."

"Why not?"

"Because it's too damn noisy, that's why," he snapped.

Footsteps outside prevented Trini from asking another question. People congregated outside on the wide, wooden landing. Trini shot an inquiring look at her father, who avoided her gaze by opening the cash register and organizing the change in the drawer. When nearly a dozen people had gathered, talking loudly all the while, they disappeared into the neighboring store, which was odd because her father owned it and the last she heard, it was vacant.

"What's going on over there?" she asked.

"Oh, the usual," her father replied vaguely.

Trini regarded him through narrowed eyes. He wasn't usually so tight-lipped. She'd have to investigate for herself. "I'll be right back," she called over her shoulder as she hurried out the door.

When she entered the former liquor store—which had gone out of business after most of the thirsty residents of Palo Verde had left—it was filled with people settling down at a long table, getting ready to make protest signs by the looks of it.

She knew most of them, even though she didn't know all their names. Holdouts. The most stubborn of the stubborn. Rose Delgado, who lived around the corner, was showing off her sign, which read, "Save our homes and our freedom!" She had hair the color of pearls fixed up in a towering bouffant. A feisty woman if there ever was one. With a career as a Spanish translator downtown, she'd never married and shared her opinions freely—especially anything involving the eminent domain evictions.

As people noticed Trini's presence, the room grew quieter, but she hardly noticed because the young man sitting at the far end of the table had all her attention. Bobby Guerra. Better looking than ever in a crisp white shirt that showed off his bronze skin and dark hair. He was regarding her with amusement, which annoyed the hell out of her. At least her flannel skirt covered her banged up knees.

"What are you doing here?" she asked across the length of the room.

Bobby's smile broadened to a grin. "Hello to you, too, Trini. We're getting ready for a meeting tonight. The city isn't letting the public in on this one, but we need to make our presence known. You know, keep up the pressure."

Trini could not care less about that. Everybody had gone back to talking and painting signs. She walked up to Bobby. "I meant, why are you in my dad's place?" she asked, tapping a foot.

At this, Bobby leaned back in his chair and cocked an eyebrow. "I'm renting it. We're using this space for our meetings, and if you'll remember, there's the apartment in the back, so I've moved in." He hesitated. Lowering his voice, he added, "And it's right next door to your father, so I can watch out for him if he needs anything." The answer caught Trini by surprise.

Bobby got to his feet. Standing so close, she noticed his height. He was at least four inches taller than she was. Five-foot seven meant she often had to wear flat shoes on dates, not that she went out much. He took her elbow and guided her outside. She was too surprised to protest.

The setting sun had turned the sky a fiery orange. Bobby leaned against the building and stared at the pink-tinted clouds. He had a high-bridged nose that gave him a dramatic profile. She eyed him warily.

Finally, he spoke. "The meeting is supposed to be short, not even an hour, so I won't be gone long. Can you stay until I get back? So your father isn't home alone?"

Trini stared up at him in astonishment. "You're kidding?"

Bobby crossed his arms in front of his chest and shook his head. "I'm not. I think you've heard something funny has been going on. Some of the old people are spooked, especially your father. There are all kinds of crazy rumors going around. That's why I moved back, to tell you the truth, to see for myself. Look, I've got to go if we're going to make it to the meeting, but you'll stay? Till I get back?" She wondered if the rumors had anything to do with the figure in white she saw lurking around earlier in the day.

She swallowed, then nodded. She had lots of questions, but now was not the time to ask. "Sure." Then she surprised herself by adding, "I'm making my father dinner. I'll fix an extra plate for you."

Bobby smiled. "Really? Wow. Some dinner would be great. Thank you, Trini."

Trini took extra care fixing dinner, as her father sat reading a newspaper at the kitchen table. Luckily, he had everything she needed in the store to make Chili Colorado.

While the dish simmered, she inspected the house. Like the store, it could use a good dusting, but otherwise, everything was neat and tidy. Trini hated mess and clutter. She grabbed a rag and wiped down the furniture. It didn't take long—there were two bedrooms and a small living room. The best part of the house was the back porch which overlooked a yard and, beyond it, a view of Elysian Park. Some days, she could see horses and goats roaming the hills. She was tempted to sit out and have a smoke in the fresh air, but then, she remembered the dog-faced creep in the wood. What if the trickster had followed her?

Over dinner, she tried asking her father what was bothering him, but he clammed up, which worried her more than anything he could have said. He had never been one to pass up an opportunity for drama. As always, he complained she hadn't made the food spicy enough, but she didn't want to burn off Bobby's tongue by serving it as hot as her father preferred. At least he was eating. She gave him a few extra flour tortillas with butter. He needed fattening up.

When they had finished their meal, she ordered him to take a hot shower, with specific instructions to wash his hair.

"Bossy, just like your mother," he muttered as his chair scraped against the wooden floor. Before going down the hall, he made a big show of locking the doors and making sure all the windows were closed and latched.

She washed the dishes at the sink. Outside, it was eerily quiet. No kids calling to each other as they played their games, no men coming home after a long day at work in the city below, no women sitting together on benches, darning, and gossiping in the fast-fading light. Not a single soul. The stillness filled her with unease. Now that she was back, she understood how the place could get under your skin, and it would only get worse. Some of the holdouts would crack under the pressure and sell up, and the number of residents would continue to dwindle.

She gave herself a shake and set about making hot chocolate. When her father finally emerged from the bathroom, she ordered him to bed and brought two mugs, fragrant with cinnamon and chocolate, and set them on the nightstand.

"Are you going to sit there staring at me," he grumbled, pulling up the green Chenille bedspread.

Trini pushed his feet aside to make room and plopped down at the end of the bed. "Yes. I'm going to sit here until you tell me what's been happening that you wanted me to come home right away."

He glared at her over his mug. "I don't need to tell you a damn thing." He paused. "Is it too much to ask to see my only daughter?"

She was thinking this over when there was a knock at the door. Her father startled so violently the hot chocolate splashed everywhere, including Trini's flannel skirt. With a sigh, she plucked the cup from her father's trembling hand and went to answer the door.

It was Bobby Guerra. "How's the old man?" he asked, keeping his voice low.

"Cranky and jumpy," she said. "Your plate is in the kitchen," she added, suddenly feeling shy.

He smiled. "I'm starving, thank you, but hey, you need to get going." He pointed over his shoulder, where a car idled at the curb. "Rose said she'd drive you home. We don't want you trying to walk out of here in the dark on your own."

Trini was tempted to remind him she knew how to take care of herself, but then, she remembered the weirdo in the woods and thought the better of it, and she didn't want Bobby to think she didn't know how to be gracious.

She cleared her throat and returned his smile. "Thank you," she said stiffly.

"Be back tomorrow?" he asked as he headed into the kitchen. Did she detect a hopeful note in his voice?

"Maybe," she said. "I'm working tomorrow. It depends on whether Henry needs me to close up." Then she went to her father, who had changed into a fresh set of pajamas, and said her goodbyes, explaining Rose would drive her back to Boyle Heights.

"Be careful," he said gruffly. Then he crossed himself. "Vaya con Dios." Trini's eyes snapped open. She couldn't remember a time when her father sent her off with a blessing.

She got into Rose's car and waved at Bobby, who stood in the doorway, dinner plate in hand. As they drove down the dirt road past Bertita's house, she spotted the old woman in her brimmed cap standing in her front yard, accompanied by Lencha and a few young men carrying sheets of plywood. Bertita was waving her cane around, supervising the boarding up of the windows.

Chapter 5

Trini spent her afternoon break throwing darts behind the market, trying to get her mind off Dog-Face bride she'd seen up in Chavez Ravine. She wasn't prone to nightmares, but it haunted her dreams and, by the morning, was sure of two things. She had not imagined it, and it had possessed the unmistakable shape of a woman. How it came to have the face of a dog, she couldn't say, but if it was a mask, it was an awfully good one.

Trini also had the nagging feeling she was being left out of something important, like those rumors Bobby mentioned. She'd had no luck getting her father to talk about whatever was upsetting him, and she'd even tried pumping Rose Delgado for information on the drive home, but the woman had quickly changed the subject.

She studied her grouping with a critical eye. Throwing darts was nowhere near as fun as shooting a gun, but even Ripper—who'd taught her everything she knew about darts, slingshots, and guns—would have to admit she threw like a pro.

The back door of the market flew open. Henry Loya stood there, wild-eyed. Trini's heart felt like it had jumped into her mouth. "Henry. What is it?"

Henry flapped a hand in her general direction. "It's your father. Get your things. I'll drive you."

Trini suddenly felt faint. Nothing bad had ever happened to her father, despite his many complaints. "Oh, my God. Is it serious?"

Henry took off his glasses and cleaned them with a corner of his green apron, blinking. "I think so. I had a hard time understanding Rose, she was talking so fast on the phone. She said someone jumped him and messed him up pretty bad."

Trini stared at her boss. "Someone jumped him!" she echoed. "My dad? Why? Where?"

Henry shook his head. "I don't know, but we should go."

The next thing she knew, she was sitting next to Henry Loya in his new Chevrolet Bel Air. They drove in silence up Whittier Boulevard, past Skid Row, Fifth, and Broadway and through Chinatown. Had someone tried to rob her father at the store? Beat him for whatever cash he had in the register? In all the years he'd owned the market, such a thing had never happened. It didn't make sense. Everyone in Chavez Ravine knew the store was barely making it with so many people gone.

When they arrived at her house, Bobby Guerra was waiting out front along with Rose and Bertita. Trini flung open the car door and ran toward them.

"What happened?" she asked.

The three exchanged looks. She didn't like this one bit. "What is it? Please, tell me," she snapped. She wasn't in the mood to put up with evasions and nonsense, and she didn't think she could stand one more second of not knowing the truth, no matter what it was.

Bertita gave a tight nod. "Your father went for a walk this morning. He asked Rose to cover for him at the store—"

Rose interrupted. "Since you're not around anymore, Trini, he asks for a little favor once in a while." Bertita shot Rose a disapproving look.

26

Rose made a face. "Well, he does, doesn't he?"

Bertita ignored this and continued. "When he didn't come back, Rose got worried, and then he was gone a whole hour. Then two."

"He's never gone for more than half an hour," Rose put in helpfully, undeterred by Bertita's scowl.

"When Bobby got back from the city, he went looking for him, but no luck, so he got some people to help search for him. They found him in the woods. You know the place where the kids like to play in between here and Loma."

Trini's heart began hammering in her chest. The same place she'd seen the dog-faced woman.

For the second time in two days, Bobby Guerra took her by the elbow, this time gently guiding her into her own house. Her father was lying in his bed, a tall and familiar figure at his side. Dr. Eng, the family doctor from Chinatown. She felt a rush of relief at seeing him there.

Her father's face was gray and clammy, a bandage wrapped around his head. His eyes remained closed as she gazed down at him. Terrible scratches covered his bare neck and chest. His right leg stuck out from underneath the sheet, propped up on a pillow, the knee so swollen it appeared misshapen.

She turned to Dr. Eng. "Is he going to be okay?" she asked faintly. She could feel Bobby standing behind her.

Dr. Eng hesitated, long enough so that Trini felt a clutch of fear. "I'm not sure what happened to him out there," he began in his rich, deep voice. "He was unconscious when they found him. Whoever did this roughed him up pretty bad." He paused. "I've got some bad news, Trini. Your father's had a heart attack. That's what I'm most concerned about. He'll need lots of bed rest to recover. And he won't be able to run the store by himself, and he'll need someone to take care of him." Then he stopped, staring down at her with an expectant expression.

Trini squeezed her eyes shut, feeling the weight of his words crushing down on her. The man might as well have saddled her with wet sandbags. There went her job at Loya's Market. There went her sweet little cottage and all her privacy. She'd have to quit college, at least temporarily. There would be no time to study between minding the market and taking care of her father, but she didn't have a choice. Her brother had a job and a family of his own in Pico Rivera, and besides, no one ever expected men to help in these kinds of situations.

As she digested all this, she was vaguely aware of voices in the hall outside her father's bedroom. When she turned, she saw Henry and Bobby deep in conversation. Both men entered a few moments later.

"I'm sorry, Henry," she said. "But my dad needs me. I guess this means I'll need to leave my job."

Henry made a clucking noise. "We were talking about that. You can have the job back when you're ready. If you still want it, and your place, too. You're like family, Trini." He squeezed her hand. "You stay with your father as long as you need to."

"And I can help you, Trini," Bobby added.

"Thank you, both of you," she said with a rush of gratitude that threatened to overwhelm her. Then, after a moment's consideration, she added, "And you can start by telling me what the hell is going on around here."

Chapter 6

As soon as Trini started firing off questions, Henry offered to drive home and have his wife pack her things. Trini accepted gratefully. Besides, he didn't seem to know much about the weird happenings in Chavez Ravine anyway.

She listened carefully as Dr. Eng explained how to care for her father. After seeing him off, she went in search of Bobby Guerra. She spotted him down the street in front of Bertita's house.

As usual, a small group of people surrounded him. They turned to stare at her as she approached. They were familiar faces: Bertita, a kind busybody and oldest inhabitant of Palo Verde, Lencha the curandera, who some people swore was a witch, Rose Delgado, who made her living as a Spanish translator downtown, and Martin Bernal. The man owned lots of property in the three neighborhoods of Chavez Ravine. It was rumored the City of Los Angeles had to send Martin more than a dozen eviction notices.

They bombarded her with questions, most of which she couldn't answer. Like them, she had no idea who or what caused her father's injuries.

Trini saw no point in beating around the bush. "Why did you board up the windows?" she asked Bertita.

"Ai, Trini," said Rose, a pinched look on her face. "She and Lencha are all alone in that big house. They need a little extra protection."

If everyone kept talking like this, she was going to scream. "Protection from what? Exactly?" Trini demanded.

A screeching noise began in the distance. The racket made Trini wince, but no one else appeared bothered by it. From the sound of it, it was coming from Bishop, the neighborhood nearest to downtown.

"It's the fire department," said Bobby, frowning. "They've been setting fire to some homes down there. The city is killing two birds with one stone. Fire training and demolition." He paused and clenched his fists. "It's the city's way of sending a message to the holdouts. We will burn you out if you don't leave, another one of their damned intimidation tactics."

"And don't forget all the other stuff they're up to!" Bertita said, shaking her cane in the air.

Trini whirled around to face Bobby. "Can you please explain what is going on around here? All of you know something you're not telling me."

Bobby blinked and held out both his hands, palms facing outward. "Okay, okay, I'm sorry. I keep forgetting you haven't been around. We think the city is getting desperate. Desperate enough to take drastic measures to get everyone to sell up because nothing else has worked. They've tried threatening people with the police, saying they'd be arrested if they don't leave. They've tried sending thugs threatening to condemn properties, and now, they're running their sirens and burning houses. They're working their way up the hill in Bishop." As if on cue, the siren started up again.

Martin moved closer to Trini, so close the brim of his fedora nearly touched her face. "They're trying to scare us out. We've all seen things. Weird things. One night, this lady showed up in my backyard. I got my flashlight and went out there. You know, to make sure she was okay. So when I shined the light on her, she gave me a real susto. The bitch had the face of a dog, but I'm the only one who's seen it."

He was dead wrong, but she wasn't ready to talk about it. Not yet. Trini did her best to hide her alarm and thought she'd pulled it off until she noticed Bobby watching her.

Bertita said, "Boogeymen have started coming at night. They stand at the front of the house, staring, and they make the most awful noises…" Her voice trailed off as she regarded the boarded-up windows. "That's why we put those up. To make sure they don't get in."

Trini shook her head, hardly able to believe her ears. The old lady might be nosy, but she wasn't the type to exaggerate.

Rose took off a heeled shoe and rubbed her foot, leaning against Martin for support. "I heard something moving around on my porch, real late at night, and when I looked out the window, I saw a man. Hairy and naked. He was real short, but the cojones on him! He stayed out there until I called Martin and he drove over with his rifle."

Despite her growing alarm, Trini made a mental note Rose had a phone at her house—it might come in handy. Few people in Chavez Ravine had phones, including her father, who had refused to put one in, calling it a luxury he could not afford.

Martin sighed. "By the time I got there, the man was gone."

Trini rubbed the side of her face. "This doesn't make sense. The city could *make* all of you go. Send in the police and arrest you or something for ignoring the eviction notices."

"I'm not so sure it's the city," Lencha put in. "Those things are sent from the devil himself." Then she turned and walked toward the house, her long black braid stark against the white of her dress.

Bertita sniffed. "She's going to make more of her powders. I think you should sprinkle some around your house, Trini, in case whatever it is that attacked your father comes back to finish him off."

Trini's eyes widened. She shot a swift glance at Bobby, who shrugged.

"That's okay," she said uneasily. Lencha, she knew, was superstitious. Besides her famous cures, she also believed in spells, curses, and demons, and El Diablo himself.

"Suit yourself," Bertita said. "You can always send Bobby over if you change your mind." Then, with a meaningful look at the two of them, she turned on her heel and went into the house. Trini cringed with embarrassment.

After assuring Martin and Rose she would be fine on her own with her father, Trini and Bobby wandered up the dirt road. They said an awkward goodbye and went their separate ways; Bobby to his apartment to work on a speech for a labor union meeting and Trini to check on her father. He was still asleep. Dr. Eng had warned her he might not wake at all until the morning.

Salvio's skin color remained a worrisome shade of gray, but at least he was breathing normally. She gingerly lifted the sheet and inspected the scratches on his chest. Ugly, raw, and deep, made by something sharp and nasty. Dr. Eng couldn't say what had made them, and no matter how many times she'd asked, he'd refused to guess. But he hadn't been able to hide the worry in his dark eyes as he'd gazed down at his patient, eyebrows furrowed.

She thought of the dog-faced woman in white, the same one that had visited Martin. Had she—it?—attacked her father on his walk? Did it even have hands? Or paws? Who knew what was hidden under the sleeves of its long dress? For all she knew, it was some thug from the city dressed up in a costume and had gone after her father with a hand rake. A knock at the door interrupted her dark train of thoughts.

It was Henry Loya with her things. When they'd finished moving the cardboard boxes into the house, he handed her a warm dish of enchiladas.

"Esther is a saint," Trini said, smiling as she peeked under the foil. Henry's wife had made them the way she liked, with extra cheese, topped with green onions and olives. "I'm about to make a fresh pot of coffee. Want a cup?"

Henry shook his head. He took off his black frame glasses and rubbed the lens with a corner of his sweater. "No, I better get back. But, Trini, listen to me. You be careful, alright? How about I go talk to Bobby? See if he can come over and sleep on the couch. You know. It might be a good idea to have a man around the house."

Trini suppressed a smile at the thought of Bobby protecting her. His ability to smooth talk had its limits. She didn't think it would work on boogeymen.

She patted his arm. "We'll be fine, Henry. I'll make sure the doors are locked." Standing on the front porch, she watched him get in his Bel Air and drive off. She shivered. The sky had turned a weird, muddy red, and the wind was rising.

She went inside and put everything away in her bedroom, but not before changing into overalls, mopping the floor, and wiping out the drawers. Then she went to the hall closet, found fresh sheets, and made her bed, smoothing the yellow bedspread until all the wrinkles were gone. Still restless, she decided she might as well get started on the market. She ate two of the enchiladas without bothering to warm them up. When she finished her simple meal, she made fresh coffee, took a cup, and walked next door to Duran Market & Liquor.

Inside, she turned on all the lights, then grabbed a box cutter from a drawer. She checked the back rooms to make sure no one—or no thing—was hiding, ready to jump out when her back was turned. The back door was locked, but, as an extra precaution, she shoved a couple of heavy barrels in front of it.

She drank her coffee while she cleaned, starting with washing the big plate glass window. Outside, the wind lifted the dirt from the road into the air. It was unnaturally quiet.

The houses directly across from the market, once home to two big families, were empty, their windows dark. Her father remained, and Bertita and Lencha down the street. Rose was around the block. Martin Bernal lived in Loma. There had to be other people around. She didn't know where exactly. Had the viejitos gone? She'd forgotten about the old men—gringos—who lived in rows of shacks on the road leading out of La Loma and into Solano. One of them had taught history at the college, before he developed a drinking problem. The professor, everyone used to call him. A nice man. He used to help her and the other kids with their homework. Later, Trini would stop by to hear his stories about Sonoratown and the early days of Los Angeles when it was a Spanish outpost.

She turned her back on the empty road—sad and desolate— and began dusting the shelves. When she was done, she rearranged the items to her liking and unpacked several boxes of canned foods. Then she stood back, rubbing her lower back, and surveyed the results. Better, but there was still plenty of work to do.

When she glanced at the window, she saw with surprise it was dark out. Not completely, though. A faint reddish glow remained, and the wind had become so strong it rattled the door. Bobby Guerra was next door. She could knock, and he'd walk her home if she asked. But that was ridiculous. Her house was a short way from the store. Still, it wasn't worth taking any chances.

She grabbed her father's gun from the drawer, made sure it was loaded, then left.

Chapter 7

A noise startled Trini awake. It sounded like a tree branch scratching against one of the front windows. Probably the wind. It had been blowing hard when she'd drifted off, and then she remembered there were no trees near the house—the closest one was across the street.

The scratching continued, louder now. Trini slipped out of bed, pulled overalls on top of her pajamas, and crept down the hall. After a few feet, she stopped and ran back to her room, snatching up the gun from the bedside table and shoved it into the toy holster she'd dug out of a cabinet before she'd gone to bed. She'd had it since she was a kid, back when her hero was Annie Oakley. Still was. A flashlight would be handy, but the only one in the house needed new batteries.

At the door to the living room, she paused, heart hammering. No mistake. The sound was coming from outside. She'd pulled the curtains shut, so she had no way of seeing what was out there, but she had to find out. She crossed the room in her bare feet and peaked out of the crack between the two curtain panels.

A figure in white stood on the porch with its back to her, the long veil flapping like a sail in the wind. The Dog-Face Bride she'd seen in the wood. She closed her eyes, shivering. It was out there. It wasn't her imagination.

"Martin saw it, too," she murmured, pressing fingers to her forehead.

Her muscles began to twitch with electric prickles of fear. The doors and windows were locked, she reminded herself. If it tried to get in, she'd hear it with enough time to aim and shoot. She backed out of the room as fast as she could and slipped into her father's room. He was still sound asleep. At least, she didn't have to worry about him. For now.

They didn't have a phone, so she couldn't call Martin to come over with his rifle. The closest person was Bobby, unarmed and next door. She crouched in the darkness of the hallway, thinking over her situation. Stuck. That's what she was.

A terrible shrieking came from outside in the distance. "Christ," she moaned. "What the hell is that?"

She felt like running, but she had nowhere to go, not with that thing on the porch. The panic was mounting. She needed to see what all the screaming was about, and fast.

Then she remembered the attic.

She pulled on the cord dangling from the ceiling and lowered the ladder, scrambling up the steep steps into the inky blackness. She crawled to the little window over the side door of the house. From her vantage point, she could see all the way to the end of the short street. She opened the window a few inches. The moon was so bright it was clear what was making all the noise: tall figures, skinny bare legs and arms sticking out from hooded robes. Six of them near Bertita's house. So pale, they were nearly white, the hoods obscuring their faces. They directed their long, piercing screams at the house, and they were jumping so high in the air; it looked like they were bouncing on trampolines.

A freak show if ever she saw one. Maybe that's what they were. Circus freaks hired by the city to scare them.

"What the hell is going on?" she muttered, putting a shaky hand to her head.

The beam of a flashlight slid across her face.

Bobby. He was standing on the roof of the apartment, waving to get her attention. Just what they needed. To become a target for the jumpers.

"Are you crazy?" she hissed. "Go back inside!"

"Are you okay?" he called quietly.

She could hear the wind. It whipped through the trees lining the ridge, rattled the tin roofs of the sheds behind the abandoned houses, and whistled across the telephone wires criss-crossing the road. She was about to order him back inside, using the tone of voice she reserved to order around the stock boy at Henry's market, when a new sound assaulted her ears.

Screams. Only one lady had a loud enough voice to be heard from around the block. Rose Delgado. "Help me. Madre mia de Dios. Help me." There was no mistaking her pleas for help.

Bobby flicked off his flashlight. "Trini. I need to go. Stay inside with your dad."

Trini felt a clutch of fear. He wouldn't make it halfway down the street. The Dog-Face Bride would get him. Even if it didn't, the weird jumpers would, and whatever else was out there, waiting in the dark.

"I'm going with you," she announced, surprising even herself.

Slowly and with exaggerated movement, he shook his head. Then, as sure-footed as a goat, he made his way across the roof and disappeared into the attic window.

There was nothing left to do but go after the man.

She slid down the attic steps and, as quietly as she could, ran across the living room. The thing in white was still out there, lurking at the far corner of the porch. Now was her chance. She rushed into the kitchen, slid her feet into her work boots, opened the side door, and ran out. Then she bolted down the street toward the market. Bobby was coming around the side of the building.

When he swung into the road, he stopped and shouted, "Trini! Watch out! Behind you!"

When she whirled around, she found herself staring into the glittering black eyes of a growling dog. The eyes were new, but the rest was familiar enough—the tall figure in white, the tattered veil. When she'd seen the figure in the wood, it had been perfectly still. Now, it was quivering all over and looked ready to leap.

Reaching into the holster—thank God she'd taken the time to oil the leather—she pulled out the gun. She'd never shot anything besides tin cans and the occasional squirrel, and if it were some pendejo in a costume out to scare them, she'd end up in jail. Or worse.

With a growl, the Dog-Face Bride lunged toward them. Trini fired. There was a flicker. It lasted a moment so short her eyes barely registered it, and then the creature continued to stand as if nothing had happened. She knew the gun had gone off. She'd felt its kick.

She aimed again.

This time, she didn't bother to stick around to check the results. She spun around and sprinted toward a stunned-looking Bobby and dragged him up the street—away from Bertita's and the jumpers—and along a skinny path between two houses that served as a shortcut to Rose's street.

They stopped briefly, ducking behind a giant nopales cactus, and scanned the area. At least, they weren't being followed. It's possible she'd hurt the thing after all. Then they continued to run, using the sound of Rose's screams to guide them. When they came to her house, Trini saw the cause of all the ruckus. A short and heavy naked man was throwing himself at the front door. It was a good thing the high porch was so narrow because he didn't have the space to get up the speed to do much damage.

Trini looked over at Bobby. For the first time, she noticed he was carrying a bat, as if he knew how to use it.

She glanced nervously over her shoulder. Still no sign of the Dog-Face Bride. The jumpers were still at it around the block. She could hear their piercing cries loud and clear.

Without bothering to consult Bobby, she shouted, "Hey, you, crazy man! Get away from that door, or I'm going to shoot." She heard Bobby's swift intake of breath beside her.

The naked man stopped his bashing and whirled around.

Trini kept her eyes above its belly button. She'd already seen enough to know he was built like a bull. And hairy as a dog. Disgusting. And what the hell was wrong with his face? A giant, down-turned bulbous nose, a gaping mouth, and eyes so far apart, they were practically on the side of his face. Calling it ugly didn't do it justice. Even from a distance, Trini could smell him, like something rotting.

He pawed the wooden porch like a bull getting ready to charge. Trini felt her hand tremble as she lifted the gun, ready to fire, but instead of springing toward them, he turned and thudded down the porch and hurled himself over the railing with surprising agility, disappearing into the darkness.

"And don't come back!" Trini shouted after him, her voice shaking.

The front door slowly opened a few inches. Rose peered through the crack, wearing her robe and curlers, her face white. "God bless you, Trini," she said. Then noticing Bobby, she added, "And to you too, young man. I tried calling Martin, but my phone isn't working."

41

"We're going to check on Bertita," Trini said. "It looks like she's got some weird visitors, too. I think whatever Lencha did seems to be working because they aren't going near her house, but we better check, just in case."

Rose nodded. She looked worn out and small in the dim light of the porch. Trini hated to leave her. Then she remembered she'd left her father alone in the house, without knowing what had happened to the Dog-Face Bride. What if it had all been a trick to lure her away so it could finish off her father. She told Bobby, and his eyes widened. Together, they ran through the darkness back to the house. There was no sign of the terrible creature in white. When they went inside, they found her father asleep and snoring, all the doors and windows still safely secured.

The wind tearing at their clothes, they darted across the street and cut through a side yard of an empty house and hopped a few fences so they could sneak up on Bertita's without being seen. A rickety lean-to shed provided some cover. They hid, watching the tall, white figures, still jumping impossibly high.

"Who the hell are they, Bobby?" she whispered.

Whoever was behind all this, they'd gone through a whole lot of trouble to scare them, and it was working. Because, as much as she hated to admit it, she was frightened.

Bobby sighed. "Well, if Lencha's right, that's where these things are from. Hell. Compliments of El Diablo himself."

Trini stared at him, incredulous. She had to admit, even at a time like this, the guy had a way with words.

Chapter 8

Trini woke early. She hadn't slept much, but two cups of strong, black coffee fixed that. It didn't solve her other problem, which was her father, moaning and thrashing around. Offering soothing words and nursing old men didn't come naturally, but she did her best. She brought in a bowl of warm water and gave him a sponge bath.

Her father resisted her attempts to get him to eat, but he drank some water before his eyes fluttered closed, and he fell back asleep. It was a miracle he'd slept through all the hollering and shrieking that had gone on overnight. She wondered if Bobby was up yet. When they'd finally stumbled home, he'd insisted on keeping watch in the living room but, by seven o'clock, he'd gone. At least, he'd left a note. "The ladies are fine. I checked. Went back to my place to sleep. Knock when you're up."

She planned on it as there was a lot to discuss, but not before taking a hot bath in the clawfoot tub. She wished there was some bubble bath but soaking in the steaming water was enough to relax her tense muscles. When the water cooled, she put her head under the faucet and turned on the tap. Cold water helped tame her wavy hair.

After all the running around in overalls and boots, and considering the boogeymen would probably return, there was no point putting on a skirt and nice shoes. Or fixing her hair. She had no patience for pin curls, not after the night she had.

Instead, she dressed in a pair of dungarees and a checked shirt. Then she combed out her dark hair, parted it down the middle and made two loose braids, a style she'd seen in a magazine. She grabbed the gun, stuck it in the toy holster and tucked it into her waistband.

Checking on her father one last time, snoring again, she walked to Bobby's apartment and banged on a side window as she passed. He was waiting at the back door when she got there, slumped against the doorway, eyes drooping with fatigue, and wearing nothing but his pajama bottoms. He had some muscles, she noted with surprise. She lifted her eyebrows. Looking down at his bare stomach, he made a funny little noise and disappeared.

Minutes later, he reemerged wearing flannel pants and a black sweater, except he hadn't put on a shirt, leaving his chest exposed. She decided against pointing this out. No sense in embarrassing the man.

"You still think it's the city trying to scare us out?" she asked as she followed him into the tiny kitchen.

Bobby stopped mid-stride and turned to stare at her. "Hey. In case you didn't notice, you said 'us.'"

"Simmer down, Bobby," she said flatly. "It's just a matter of speech."

"I don't know anymore. About the city. Not after last night." He sank into a chair. "It's kind of hard to imagine, even for those idiots, but if it's not them, then who else could it be?"

Trini spotted a loaf of bread on the counter, so she busied herself making toast and coffee. Bobby didn't protest. He sat at the table, staring at his hands.

"Usually, the most obvious answer is the right one," she said. "You said the ladies were okay. That means you checked on them. Any sign of the boogeymen?"

"No. It's like they were never there." Bobby's voice wavered. "Rose said the hairy man didn't come back, and you shot at that thing in white, I saw you. I don't understand how you didn't kill it, and, all night, I kept wondering why it didn't chase us."

She'd wondered the same thing, one of the many disturbing thoughts that had kept her awake. She poured them each a cup of coffee, buttered the toast, and slid a plate in front of Bobby. "Is this only happening around here in Palo Verde? Has anyone else said anything? Any people from Loma and Bishop?"

"Not in Bishop. They're closest to town, so that could have something to do with it, but in Loma, I've heard people say stuff, but mostly like seeing whirlwinds, or weird lights and noises. Martin said he thought it was the coyotes getting brave and coming down from the hills because there aren't many people around to scare them away."

Trini frowned, thinking. "Bobby, how many people are left in Chavez Ravine?"

"I don't know exactly. Around two hundred."

Trini ate her toast in silence. When she finished, she said, "My dad never told me what had him so scared. Did he tell you?"

Bobby returned her gaze over the top of his cup. "Yes, but if I tell you, can you please keep it to yourself? He told me in private."

Trini felt a flash of irritation her father had confided in Bobby. Then again, she hadn't made herself available, so she only had herself to blame. "I won't say a word," she promised.

Bobby drained the rest of his coffee and set down the cup. "You know how his mother went senile?"

Trini nodded. As if anybody could forget. The entire family had to take turns watching the woman to make sure she stayed out of trouble, not to mention listening to her crazy stories.

Bobby continued. "Well, it scared him it might run in the family, that it might happen to him, too, because he thought he was imagining things. He was getting up the nerve to tell you. I offered to take him to Dr. Eng, but he didn't want to go, and then, he heard the ladies were seeing weird things, too, so he thought maybe there wasn't anything wrong with him after all. I needed a place to live, so I said I could be, you know, an impartial observer and—"

Trini interrupted. "He told you all that?"

"He did," Bobby said, scooping up the dishes and putting them into the sink. "He's lonely up here, with you kids, gone."

Trini remembered Bobby's father was no longer alive, killed by a burst appendix a few years back. His mother, she'd heard, had moved in with her sister in Lincoln Heights. She bet Bobby was a dutiful son who visited his mom several times a week. Guilt pressed in on her chest, heavy as an elephant. She knew of one way to get rid of it. Action.

She exhaled loudly, pushed her shoulders back, and stood up. "We need to figure out who else may have seen something last night," she announced. "How about I take Loma? You take Palo Verde?"

Bobby bit his lip, considering. Finally, he said, "Like a survey. Yeah, that's a good idea." He hesitated. "But stick to the roads, okay?" He grabbed his hat and strode toward the door.

"Bobby," she called after him, grinning. "You might want to put a shirt on first."

After Lencha arrived to sit with her father, Trini slipped into her bedroom and reloaded the gun. Then, she pulled on a long sweater that covered the toy holster and headed out.

It was a crisp fall morning—no sign of the windstorm that had blown through the night before. At least the roads were dry. When it rained, they turned into a muddy mess. No matter how many times the residents of Chavez Ravine had asked the city to pave the dirt roads, it never got done, one of the many bitter complaints she'd heard growing up.

She made her way out of the Palo Verde neighborhood, hardly recognizable with so many people gone. The ramshackle houses her mother used to point out—heaping scorn on the negligent landlords—appeared to tilt, porches sloping, paint peeling. The small wood and stucco house that belonged to the Cruz family was as neat as ever. Mrs. Cruz was outside, painting the fence. She lifted her head as Trini approached.

Trini picked up her pace, gave a friendly wave, and said a brisk, "Good morning, Mrs. Cruz!" then rushed past before the woman could stop her. She didn't want to get bogged down in a conversation.

The few people she saw on the rest of her walk through Palo Verde got the same treatment. Once, a man whose name she forgot yelled, "Traitor!" as she sped by.

La Loma wasn't any different—more dilapidated, empty houses, overgrown yards strewn with metal wash tubs and broken chairs, no kids, no dogs.

A door flew open, making Trini jump and startling the crows in a tree. They squawked in protest and flew off. A man around her age appeared wearing a white t-shirt, black pants, and a gray beanie. Pete Chavira. She was surprised to see him—she hadn't seen many young people around.

Pete did a double take when he spotted her. "What are you doing here, Trini? I'd heard you'd got out. Left this dump."

Trini pursed her lips. As much as she'd been eager to leave Chavez Ravine, she hated hearing people criticize it, especially people like Chavira. "Hey, Pete, you're up early. On your way to steal some cars?"

Pete ignored this. His eyes flicked over her. "Why you dressed like that?"

Trini rolled her eyes. "Nothing wrong with being comfortable, Pete." If she was going to talk to him, it might as well be about something useful. She forced herself to give him a friendly smile. "That was some crazy wind last night, right? I thought the roof was going to come off."

Pete strolled across the yard toward her. Her friend Weechie had a big crush on him back in high school. She had to admit Pete was a nice-looking guy, if you could put up with his personality and bad habits. He had a scar above his lip. Knife fight, she'd heard.

"I didn't hear anything," he said.

"Drink too much?" she asked.

He crossed his arms in front of his chest. "I gave that up. Going straight." He lifted his chin. "I've got a job, at the brickyard, and I'm boxing. Ripper's teaching me." His eyes gleamed with admiration. Ripper had that effect on men.

Before he could start going on about Ripper Cuevas, she said, "Congratulations on that job, Pete. Good for you. You're saying there was no windstorm here last night?"

He shook his head. "No, and I was up real late, too, reading. Why you asking?"

Trini's eyes widened. The guy was full of surprises. She was tempted to ask what he was reading, but she didn't want to prolong the conversation. "Just curious, that's all. Well, see you around, Pete."

"I'll come over and see you later," he called after her. Trini walked away stiffly, pretending not to have heard. That's the last thing she needed. Pete Chavira sniffing around, interested.

Her thoughts circled back to the windstorm, or the absence of one in Loma, according to Pete. She believed him. His ears worked fine. If the wind had been blowing, he'd have heard it. Loma wasn't far from Palo Verde, so there should have been at least a strong breeze, and if he'd seen anything weird, he would have said it. Pete wasn't the kind to hold back.

It made no sense. Then again, nothing made sense since she'd returned to Chavez Ravine.

She'd finally reached the edge of La Loma, her actual destination. She hadn't told Bobby, fearing he'd try to stop her. Some people had odd opinions of los viejitos, the old white men who lived in beat-up old shacks, and she wasn't sure where Bobby stood on the matter. She could see the homes on Amador and Solano Avenue below.

Not a sound came from the tiny cabins lining the slope. Rough-hewn wooden planks served as steps alongside them. Most of the old bachelors must be long gone. Her mother told her an old man named Mr. Sander owned the shacks and he was nice to the Mexican families, which was saying a lot because, when her mother was alive, she was very suspicious of gringos.

The streets of Los Angeles were below. Cars whizzed past. People were out on the streets, starting their day. She stood on a skinny dirt path with a small hill on one side and the wall of shacks on the other, hidden from view. The dirt path that was Phoenix Street was somewhere off to her right.

As far as she could tell, she was alone. If she screamed, no one would hear her.

Trini slipped the gun out of its holster and made her way down the steps.

The man she called the professor lived in the middle of the long row of shacks.

She made her way quietly, stepping over upturned buckets, discarded washboards, and broken wine bottles, but it was the doors that caught her attention. It looked like someone had ripped them off their hinges. The windows hadn't fared much better—punched in or pulled out. She got up the nerve to peek inside one. It was dark, but she could make out an overturned table and chairs.

She knew she ought to turn around and get Bobby, although Pete made more sense since he was closer, and tougher. Something was wrong. Something had happened, but the compulsion to investigate was too strong.

The wooden planks creaked and groaned under her feet.

The crooked little path veered sharply to the left. As she rounded the bend, hands so clammy it was making it hard to hold the gun, she shrieked.

A pair of legs stuck out of a doorway. She froze, listening so hard her temples and forehead ached with the effort. The only sound she heard was a thumping in her ears from her heart hammering in her chest. She stepped forward, eyes traveling up the trousered legs. A bald, middle-aged man. Dead. His face and neck covered in awful scratches; shirt ripped open to reveal an ugly gaping wound on his chest. Trini felt her stomach heave.

A noise began further down the row of shacks.

As Trini backed away, it resolved into the meow of an insistent cat. She hurried down the steps.

A black kitten hurled itself at her legs, making her jump. When she bent to pick it up, it darted away to a shack further down the slope. It stopped and looked over its shoulder. Clearly, the little thing wanted her to follow. She did, reluctantly. When she got to the shack, she saw with dismay the door was closed, and so were the windows. The kitten resumed its insistent meowing.

Trini knocked on the door. In response, she heard a faint moan. She tried the handle. Locked. This time, a loud, sustained groan came from inside. She eyed the door. It wasn't much more than a piece of plywood, and she was thin but strong. Holstering the gun, she took a few steps back and crashed into the door with her shoulder. It flew open.

The professor sat, legs splayed, on the floor of the dim room, his back against the far wall. He slowly raised his head and lifted a trembling hand.

"Hello, Trini," he croaked. Then he slumped over.

Chapter 9

When Trini and the professor finally reached Palo Verde, both arrived exhausted. Trini from supporting him from Loma and him from the pain of walking with a sprained ankle. His skin felt moist to the touch, and his color was off. Pale with a worrisome blue tinge. She hoped he hadn't had a heart attack on top of everything else he'd gone through. He'd told bits and pieces of the story on their walk, enough for her to piece things together.

The dead man's name was Hal. Both had remained in the shacks, long after the other old bachelors left. Most believed it was just a matter of time before the bulldozers arrived and knocked down the cabins. Hal worked as a movie extra and sometimes got small parts if he could stay sober that long. The professor didn't know Hal's last name. He'd awakened in the middle of the night to Hal's screams and other noises so terrible they made him shudder talking about them, like claws scraping across wood and guttural snorts.

Thinking a rabid coyote was attacking the man, he'd grabbed a shovel and ran to help, but, in the darkness, he'd tripped and fallen on the steps, hurting his ankle. As he lay there, a giant man emerged from Hal's cabin, blood dripping from his gaping mouth, and then the man lunged at him. The professor tried fighting him off with a shovel, but his strength was no match against his monstrous attacker. He vaguely remembered hearing voices in the street below, and lights, which could have scared off the stranger. When asked about what the man had worn, the professor could not recall, but had the impression of rags and, something like a cape.

The professor hadn't come away totally unscathed, not with those scratches on his chest—long and bloody marks. She'd wanted to run to Solano below and ask for help, but the professor had refused. He hated hospitals.

"What do you think it was?" Trini asked as they turned onto her street.

The professor squeezed his eyes shut. He had a beard, and his silver hair had grown long since she'd last seen him. "It. Now that's an interesting choice of word," he said, wincing as he hobbled along. "But I'm inclined to agree with you, Trini."

Lencha must have seen them coming because she greeted them on the dirt road.

Trini watched as Lencha's eyes widened, then locked on to the tall man struggling to stay on his feet.

"Professor!" she cried, holding her arms open, rushing toward them.

The professor came to an abrupt halt. "Lencha!" he said.

Trini blinked, confused. Did they know each other? It sure looked like it. They stood, eyes staring, unbelieving. Finally, Lencha came to her senses. She took his other arm, and said, "Let's take him to my place. He needs fixing up."

Trini cast a dubious glance at Lencha but remained silent. Trini could clearly remember the feeling of hot tomatoes covering her throat and chest when she was a little girl. Her mother had turned to Lencha for one of her remedies when Dr. Eng wasn't available. Hopefully, the curandera was better at treating wounds than she was at sore throats.

When they reached Bertita's house, she watched them disappear inside. Trini hurried to Rose's place around the block. Luckily, she was home, on her hands and knees, scrubbing the front porch.

"Whoever it was sure stank," she said when she saw Trini. "It's taken me all morning to get rid of that smell." Her platinum hair tower quivered with indignation.

"Can I use your phone, Rose?" she asked. "I need to call the police." Then she hastily explained the situation.

Rose worked at the criminal courts and had heard and seen it all, so she merely nodded. "Go ahead, honey. You know where it is."

Five minutes later, Trini walked into her father's room. He was sitting up in bed, fully awake and alert. She sank down beside him. His color had improved, she noted with relief. Lencha had bathed him, trimmed his hair, and cleaned up his wounds far better than she'd could have done. His eyes flicked over her. Then he spotted the gun in its toy holster.

"What's with the Anita Oakley outfit?" he asked, using her old nickname.

Trini sighed. Leave it to her father to make a crack about her appearance at a time like this. When she was a kid, he thought her obsession with Annie Oakley was cute, but when her interest in the sharpshooter continued into her teen years, he hadn't been so amused. And he didn't approve of girls wearing dungarees or overalls.

She patted the gun. "I was out doing patrols last night. Didn't Lencha tell you?"

"Lencha told me a whole lot of crazy things about demons and ghosts," he snapped. "I only believe half of what comes out of that woman's mouth."

"Lencha wasn't lying," she replied. "I saw them myself." Then, for good measure, she added, "And Bobby saw them, too."

Salvio Duran adjusted the position of his leg propped on the pillow, then grimaced. "Bobby's been hanging around those old ladies too much," he said sourly.

Trini got up and paced the room. "Dad, a man was killed last night at the shacks. One of los viejitos, except he wasn't old. I found the professor this morning. He got hurt pretty bad by a crazy man." She stopped pacing long enough to give him a sharp look. "Are you ready to tell me what happened to you?"

Her father shook his head. "It was a coyote."

Trini studied her father through narrowed eyes. He looked pleased with himself. "A coyote?" she scoffed. "A coyote did that to you? That's kind of funny, Dad, because they're scared of people and stay up in the hills."

He pulled the sheet up to his chin and pinched his lips together. "Things have changed around here since you left. The coyotes are everywhere. I was taking a walk and, when I bent down to tie my shoe, one jumped me."

Trini wasn't sure why her father was lying, but she knew a mentira when she heard one. Maybe Bobby was right. Maybe her father feared if he told the truth, people would think he was getting senile.

"Don't you have better things to do? Like get yourself over to the store so we can make some money?" he said with a sniff.

Trini crossed the room and kissed her father's forehead. No use continuing to question the man. It was obvious he wasn't ready to talk. "Sure, Dad," she said. She strode from the room, fingers hooked through the loops of her jeans.

"And put a skirt on, for God's sakes," he called after her. "Even Annie Oakley had the decency to wear a skirt!"

This, she ignored. Instead, she went into the kitchen and rummaged through the cupboards until she found what she was looking for. A bottle of Tequila. Then she set out for Bobby's. They might as well have a drink while making a plan for later.

The boogeymen were bound to return.

Chapter 10

Over three shots of Tequila each, Trini and Bobby had decided there was safety in numbers should the boogeymen thugs return. Which meant gathering everyone together under the same roof. Deciding which roof was trickier, but Bertita's had the obvious advantage. It was the largest house with plenty of bedrooms, but most importantly, it had boarded-up windows. It had taken some convincing, then an outright order to get her father to move for the night.

After everyone had arrived for the evening—including Rose and Martin with his rifle—Trini discovered a major drawback. With the windows covered with plywood, there was no way to see what was going on outside, and the attic did not have a dormer window.

"We'll have to make one," Trini said to Bobby as people trickled into the kitchen for dinner.

Bobby's eyebrows shot up, but he didn't ask questions. He was too busy scooping rice and beans onto plates in the serving line Rose had organized.

Bertita had made taquitos stuffed with minced beef and potatoes and was sitting back, smoking a cigar, and making everyone cough. The kitchen was spacious, like the rest of the rooms. The old lady had one of the biggest houses in Chavez Ravine. How she came to afford it was a tragic story, one never discussed with Bertita herself. She'd lost her husband and young child in a terrible accident in the city, and the company responsible had paid Bertita lots of money to keep it out of the newspapers.

Trini threw open a window—one of the few they'd board up later—to clear the smoky, still air. Then, she sat beside the professor at the long table. Her father sat across, eying the gringo with suspicion.

"Dad," Trini warned, pointing at his bowl. Lencha had made Salvio and the professor a special meal of chicken soup with rice. Food for the sick and injured. Trini thought both men had no business out of bed, but they'd insisted on joining the group for dinner.

Salvio frowned and dipped a spoon into the bowl. "I see a coyote got you, too," he said, with a nod at his dinner companion's chest, covered in bandages.

Trini and Bobby exchanged glances. They'd talked about her father's explanation for his attack. Both thought he wasn't telling the truth.

The professor dipped his head and replied, "That was no coyote, Señor Duran. You remember me, from the old days? John Miller."

Salvio set down his spoon. "Of course, I remember you. You used to live in those shacks in Loma, then moved away. I heard you came back. You should have stopped by to see me. We could've had a drink. I see you've been talking to Lencha again." He tapped a finger to the side of his head. "She has some strange ideas. Don't get me wrong. She's a damn good woman, and she's cured more than half the people around here, but when it comes to certain things, she's got some crazy notions. Before you showed up, she tried talking to me about them. Didn't you, Lencha?"

Lencha blinked, then shrugged. "You said it. I tried, but there's no use talking sense to an old fool." At this, Bertita hooted from the end of the table. Salvio rolled his eyes. Trini suppressed a smile. Only Lencha could get away with talking to her father like that.

Professor Miller rose slowly from the table. "If you'll excuse me, I think I was a little too ambitious and should have stayed in bed like my excellent nurse told me to." He smiled wanly at Lencha, who jumped to her feet and escorted him from the room.

Salvio gave a smug smile. "Well, it's just like old times. Those two back together again." Trini's eyes snapped open. Was her father suggesting the two—those two! —were romantically involved?

It was Rose's turn to caution Trini's father. "Ai, Salvio. You're terrible. You shouldn't go repeating stories."

"They are not stories," Salvio said, picking up his spoon. Then he finished his soup, refusing to meet his daughter's gaze.

Trini glanced at Bertita and Martin, noting neither looked surprised at her father's comment. Was it possible her father wasn't exaggerating for once? Something was going on between them, with Lencha falling all over herself to wait on the man.

Then it was Salvio's turn to excuse himself, although not as graciously as Professor Miller had done. Trini accompanied her father to the cot in his room. He grumbled as he got in, complaining he saw no point in having to leave his own more comfortable bed. She still hadn't told him about her experience with Dog-Face Bride and didn't plan to. The man had suffered a heart attack, and she couldn't risk upsetting him.

She looked down at him with a puzzled expression. "Dad, it wasn't a coyote, was it?"

Salvio busied himself sliding down in the cot without tipping it over. Then he pulled the cover up to his chin. "I'm not sure. To tell you the truth, I passed out after I got knocked down. But please, mija, don't tell the others, okay?"

Trini nodded. At least this was something she could understand. At the doorway, she stopped. "Can I bring you something? Some warm milk?"

Her father gave a weak smile. "No. I'm so tired I just want to sleep." He struggled to lift his head. "Trini. Listen. You should call the police about those tricksters those ladies keep talking about. If they come back tonight, they could mean business. You know, do something, like try to set the neighborhood on fire."

"I think you're right, Dad," she said. She felt an unexpected rush of affection. She blew him a kiss. "I'll talk to Bobby again, okay? Try not to worry." He nodded, closed his eyes and fell asleep.

In the kitchen, Bobby was helping Rose dish up strawberry ice cream. "My dad said he thinks we should call the police," she said, accepting a glass bowl from Bobby.

Martin spoke first. "Don't waste your time. The police are only good for one thing. Beating up Mexicans, that's what. And if you call them, what are you going to say? There's a bunch of people coming here at night acting all crazy, trying to scare us?" He leaned back in his chair and snorted. "The cops won't care. Hey, they probably hand out medals for that kind of thing."

Trini stared at Martin in surprise. It was unlike Martin to sound so bitter. Then she remembered off-duty police officers beat up his son in the Zoot Suit Riots, so it made sense.

"They wouldn't believe us even if we called them," Rose said. "I wouldn't put it past them to send some of their people to have a little fun with us. You should hear those damn officers talk about Mexicans down at the courts. Most of them think I'm white because of my hair, so they say all kinds of nasty stuff in front of me."

Bobby shifted in his chair. "You're right. No good will come from calling the police. There's a lot of tension between the city and the holdouts. They'd find a way to use it against us. Say we're making stuff up to make them look bad. Call us liars, and they've got the newspapers on their side. Those reporters would have a lot of fun with it."

Trini ate her ice cream, mulling this over. When she'd called the police earlier in the day to report the body at the shacks, she'd refused to give her name. She'd given no thought to why she'd withheld it, but she didn't completely trust the police either. While they'd never bothered her, they'd stopped her brother plenty of times for no good reason. Once, they'd thrown Beto into jail because they said they smelled alcohol on his breath. Beto never drank.

She pushed back her chair and rose to her feet. "Okay. We're on our own then. Here's what I think. I think the city has hired some professionals to scare us out. Because those people last night? There was something definitely weird about them." She paused to catch her breath. Normally, she didn't make speeches, and everyone was staring at her in surprise. She pushed on. "Have you ever been to the circus? People used to pay money to see sideshows with folks who had deformities. All those people didn't disappear because the sideshows stopped. What if the city has a way of finding people like that—tall ones, hairy ones, a lady with a dog face—and told them to put on a show? Scare the hell out of us?" She turned to Bertita and Lencha, whose mouths were open, looking at her as if they'd never seen her before. "Well? It's possible, isn't it?" she added in a louder voice than she intended.

Bobby cleared his throat. "Well, that's a lot of trouble to go through," he said, sounding uncertain. "But anything is possible."

Lencha patted her arm. "You're thinking too hard, Trini. Those things aren't what you think they are."

"Amen," put in Bertita, thumping her cane on the floor.

"Bobby said you fired two bullets at the dog lady," said Lencha. "Then how come you didn't kill it? What explains something like that?"

Trini's chin jutted out. "I must have missed."

"Our own Anita Oakley?" laughed Bertita, eyes gleaming. "I've seen you shoot a dozen tin cans in a row without missing. I don't think so, young lady."

Trini shrugged. "Maybe I lost my touch." An outright lie, but the sun was going down fast, and she was eager to get ready before any weirdos showed up. They could argue about who or what they were another time.

After many cuidates and con cuidados later, Trini and Bobby clambered up to the attic, each carting tools that might come in handy for their project. At least they could stand up in the large space. There was even a working light bulb dangling from a cord. Besides a few old chests, the room was empty. She'd picked up the hammer they'd brought up, when Bobby cleared his throat.

"What?" she asked, noting his odd expression.

"I can knock a hole in the wall, thank you very much," he said through gritted teeth.

He snatched the hammer from her hand and swung it several times, creating an open space the right height and size for them to peer through. Trini patted his arm, impressed. He gave her an exasperated look and dropped the tool to the ground.

After several more trips to gather blankets and pillows, they settled in, taking shifts to keep watch. As the night progressed, Trini became more and more tense, expecting the shuffle of approaching footsteps, the sound of strange piercing cries, the awful bellow of the short, hairy man with far apart eyes. Or worse, the sudden and silent appearance of the figure with the face of a dog. She imagined it floating upward until she could see its black glittering eyes staring back at her from the hole in the attic wall. She had to squeeze her eyes shut to rid herself of the image.

Sleep became impossible. Trini sat there, breathing hard, nerves rattling. Bobby scooted closer and put a tentative arm around her shoulder. When she didn't protest, he stroked her hair.

"Are you okay?" he whispered in the darkness.

"No," she whispered back. "Not really."

They stayed awake until the sun rose. Soon, they could hear voices coming from the kitchen below. Trini watched Bobby as he got up and stretched. He looked more handsome than he had a right to be after so little sleep.

It had been an uneventful night—a tremendous relief—but all the waiting around for something spooky to happen left her feeling nervous and unsettled. And she didn't like it one bit.

Chapter 11

Trini jumped every time the door of the market flew open. She'd nearly had a heart attack when someone banged on the glass at eight in the morning—the produce man, the one who delivered fruits and vegetables to Henry Loya's markets in Boyle Heights. Her father had stopped selling fresh produce, but Trini started stocking it again. Word spread and soon, people were making their way to the last market left in Chavez Ravine.

She greeted them with more enthusiasm than she could muster for the customers of Loya's Market. There, she was just another employee, but here, Duran Market & Liquor had her name on it.

Each customer visit had followed the same pattern. Surprise to see her back in Palo Verde, questions about her father, offhand comments about how the market had gone downhill since she'd left. After she'd rung up the items and bagged the groceries, an awkward silence or some beating around the bush. But every time, it ended the same. Stories of strange things they'd heard or seen: freaky-looking tall men; a whirlwind; glowing lights; something big spotted in a tree; unearthly screams; the shadow of a giant creeping past. Several frightened women reported seeing a short, hairy, naked man lurking in the bushes. Two older ladies mentioned demons. All this happened last night in La Loma. And most thought the City of Los Angeles was behind it.

Bobby poked his head in twice to check on her but retreated when he saw her busy with customers. She kept thinking back to last night. The way his arm felt around her shoulder, the way he'd stroked her hair. She wondered if it meant anything to him. What if he'd just felt sorry for her because she'd been so scared? In all those hours they'd spent together, he hadn't tried to kiss her once. Keeping watch was a mood killer, though.

She was so lost in thought when the door flew open, she startled violently. "Weechie!" she gasped.

As usual, her old friend looked like an advertisement in a magazine. The young woman wore a plaid dress in fall colors and black hair in a glamorous side part. When Weechie was little, she dreamed of becoming a model—until she topped out at five feet.

"People said you were back, but I couldn't believe it!" Weechie cried, rushing over and giving her a tight hug. "I can't believe what happened to your papa! How terrible! Is he okay? Did they find who beat him up?"

One thing hadn't changed in Chavez Ravine since she'd left. News still traveled fast. "I think he's sicker than he's telling me," Trini said. Rather than answer Weechie's last question, she changed the subject. "How are things going in Bishop?"

Weechie shook her head. "Not good. You know how we're way up the hill? We can see everything. It's a wreck. A lot of houses got knocked down since you left, and the fire department is burning stuff down, and everything smells like smoke. I don't know how much longer my parents can hold out. But you know them. Stubborn. They think the city is going to change its mind." Weechie paused, then lowered her voice. "My papa says Bobby Guerra moved into your apartment next door. Is that true?"

Trini nodded, frowning. "Yeah. He did."

Weechie wiggled her eyebrows. "Is he still as cute as ever? Because I swear, I've always had a crush on him."

68

The question caught her by surprise. "I don't know," she lied. "I guess."

Weechie sidestepped a few feet, batting her eyelashes as she went. "Then, I'll have to go over and see for myself! I'd ask you to sleep over my place so we can catch up, but I know you have to stay with your papa." She strolled to the door, one hand on her hip like a model at a fashion show. "I have a new job in the garment district. Seamstress! I'm working for a designer. He draws something, and I make it to see if he likes it." She whirled around, the full skirt swirling around her shapely legs. "He designed this one, and I made it for myself. Isn't it pretty?"

Trini forced a fake smile to her lips. "Yes, it's very pretty," she admitted.

After Weechie left, Trini sat down on a stool, fuming.

She could have told Weechie the truth. *She* liked Bobby and Weechie would have understood. Maybe. They'd never had a crush on the same boy before. Trini liked guys who were smart, and Weechie went for looks. She could not care less if they were boring idiots. Bobby Guerra was both and now, Weechie was next door doing who knew what.

She was thinking up an excuse to go over to Bobby's when Pete Chavira walked in, wearing dust-covered work clothes.

"How are you doing, Pete?" she asked. He looked hot and tired.

Pete went to the cold case, grabbed a bottle of coke, and popped the lid. "Remember how you were asking if we had wind in Loma, and I said no? Well, we had it plenty last night, and I wasn't able to sleep a wink. And then you know mean old Vera Lucero? Well, she showed up at my house, screaming her head off, saying she was being chased by a naked man. My dad and I went looking for him in the fucking middle of the night."

She jolted up off the stool, knocking it over. "And?"

"Well, we never found him, but we saw some other guys walking into Loma." Pete took a swig of Coke and continued. "Some real weirdos wearing hoods. It looked like they'd rubbed some white paste all over their skin. Man, I wanted to go kick their butts, I'm telling you. But my dad wouldn't let me. He said it was the city sending in the Ku Klux Klan and they'd string me up if they caught me."

Trini picked up the stool and studied Pete. He acted more irritated than scared. "Is that what they looked like to you?"

Pete shrugged. "I've never seen one, and I thought they wore white hoods, not dark ones like these guys, but what do I know? If those fuckers come back, I'll be ready for them, no matter what my dad says." He tossed the empty Coke bottle into the trash can, where it clanged against the metal sides.

Even though she expected the sound, Trini still flinched. "Pete, I don't think you should mess with them. Seriously."

Pete smirked. "You didn't see those guys. They're all skinny and pathetic."

"Pete," she said. "A man was killed yesterday at the shacks of los viejitos. Didn't you hear?"

"Yeah, I heard," Pete said, pulling a switchblade from the pocket of his work pants. "Nothing but gringos live in those shacks. And since when does the Klan kill their own kind? It was probably just one drunk killing another." He flicked open the knife and flexed an arm muscle. "And don't you worry about me, Trini. I've got these two things going for me."

Then he winked, placed a nickel on the counter, and strode out.

At five-thirty, Trini began closing, pleased with the money she'd taken in. The word had spread to the furthest neighborhood of Bishop a spiffed-up Duran Market & Liquor had reopened, because some Bishop ladies had trooped in. Trini's heart swelled at this. It was easier for them to shop in downtown than it was to walk all the way to Duran's.

When Trini asked the usual questions, not one of them had anything to say about strange sightings, although they'd heard about them from friends in La Loma and Palo Verde. They all believed the city was out to scare the holdouts into selling.

When she locked up for the night, she had the beginnings of a plan.

They needed to find out who those freaks were. They didn't show up out of nowhere. Did a special bus drop them off? A couple of cars? She couldn't imagine them taking the streetcar dressed like that. They had to be coming in from Broadway on Bishop Road.

She walked her father to Bertita's house, where everyone would stay the night again. This time, he didn't complain, because Bertita had promised to make Chilaquiles for dinner, his favorite. He brought along a box of checkers, hoping to get Professor Miller to play with him.

Once she'd seen him settled, Trini ran back to her house and changed out of her skirt and blouse and into her more practical outfit of dungarees and shirt. She was standing in front of Bobby's apartment when she remembered Weechie—all gussied up in the dress that showed off her tiny waist and perky bosom. She was tempted to change into something more alluring, but quickly ruled that out as impractical. A cute outfit wouldn't work for what she had in mind.

"You're kidding?" Bobby said after she laid it out.

They were sitting in Bobby's kitchen, the only place to talk besides the bedroom and the storefront. An old typewriter sat on the table, surrounded by papers.

"I'm not," she said. "If we can prove they're fakes, hired to scare us, then you can find a lawyer and sue them or tell one of your newspaper buddies about it so they could do a story."

Bobby frowned. "What about the old folks? We can't leave them alone all night."

"Martin's not that old," she replied. "And he's got a rifle. Besides, we won't be gone all night. Just long enough to spot them coming in, catch them getting dressed up and putting on their masks."

"Or taking off their clothes," Bobby said, then grimaced. "I'm not sure I'm up to seeing the naked fat guy again." He hesitated. "Don't take this the wrong way, but you were pretty scared last night, and I was, too. Are you sure you want to go chasing these guys?"

Trini rubbed the back of her neck. "I talked to a bunch of customers today. Everyone says the city's behind it. And you know Cheatin' Chavira? He came by, too. He and his dad saw those creeps last night in Loma. His dad thinks they're from the Ku Klux Klan." Then she explained what happened to Vera Lucero.

At this, Bobby sat back and swallowed. "You're right," he finally said. "We have to do something before someone gets hurt. I'll bring my bat. You bring your gun. I'll make sure the flashlights have batteries. We might not figure this out in one night, but we can at least get a start. Do you think they're coming in over the hill with the reservoir? The city owns the property. That would kind of make sense."

She thought for a moment, then shook her head. "There's a whole lot of nothing up there, just the hill and no trees. Everyone would see them out in the open. I've been thinking they're coming in from Solano, past the shacks in Loma. We can hide at the top of the hill. We'd have a good view from there."

Bobby's eyes widened. "Where the gringo got killed? After what the professor said? You want to go there, at night? That's the craziest thing I've ever heard!"

Trini sighed. He had a point, but she was also sure if the freaks were coming from the city, the crooked paths next to the shacks made the most sense.

"We need someone else to go with us. Someone who knows how to bust heads. Like Pete Chavira."

Bobby gave a loud snort. "The guy is a moron, and he's got a big mouth." He paused for a moment, scraping a hand through his hair. "But you're right. He's good in a fight."

With that decided, Trini made for the door before Bobby could change his mind. On her way out, she peeked inside the tiny bedroom. The bed was neatly made, and better yet, there was no sign of Weechie. Bobby hadn't even mentioned her dropping by.

At home, she cleaned her gun and oiled the holster, and wondered what those two had talked about. Weechie could charm just about anyone if she put her mind to it, and Bobby got along with everyone. A worrisome combination if there ever was one.

Chapter 12

They'd crouched in place for ten minutes, hidden in a shack keeping watch for the boogeymen, and Trini already regretted bringing Pete Chavira.

The guy wouldn't shut up, no matter how many times she'd shushed him. Bobby was so annoyed she half expected him to clobber Pete with his baseball bat, although now that they were holed up at the top of the slope of los viejitos, their weapons seemed negligible. She didn't think Pete's knives or Bobby's bat would do much good against that beast of a man who'd attacked Professor Miller. She had a gun. But the second they entered the dim shack, her hands started shaking so badly she'd stuck them in the pockets of her dungarees to keep Bobby and Pete from noticing.

In the light of day, it was easy to imagine the weirdos menacing the holdouts were nothing but hired hands of the city. Former circus freaks. Thugs who'd done jail time. Now that night had fallen, she wasn't sure. Her mind kept returning to Lencha's claim they were demons. The nagging uncertainty added to her anxiety.

Below, the streets of Los Angeles were quiet.

Occasionally, a car would drive past. Lights glowed on the porches of the houses on Amador and Solano, and hours had passed since mothers called their children home. Trini guessed it was close to midnight, and there was still no sign of the strange men.

Not a single gringo bachelor remained. Trini wondered where they had all gone.

The shack was cramped. Uncomfortable. She couldn't imagine Professor Miller fetching water in a pail from a faucet up the hill. No bathroom. The rough wooden floors creaked and groaned anytime someone moved. Still, the shacks had a certain dignity about them, much better than anything Skid Row could offer. Each man had their own place. The rent was cheap, and the fresh air plentiful.

A breeze swept across the hills and down the ravine where Trini sat hidden in the darkness as Bobby and Pete talked about baseball. They'd finished debating whether the Los Angeles Angels were a minor or major league team and were discussing the fights between the fans of the LooLoos and The Twinks, whoever they were. Trini couldn't care less but, at least they were whispering.

The wind rattled the tin roofs and tree branches scratched against the cabin.

She scooted closer to Bobby.

Pete stopped talking. She could feel him staring at her in the darkness. Finally, he said, "Hey Bobby, so what's the deal with you two? Are you going out, or what?"

Trini froze. She couldn't have opened her mouth if she tried. She felt Bobby put his hand over hers. Startled, she was about to pull it away when he gave it a firm squeeze.

"Why are you asking, Pete?" said Bobby, sounding amused, keeping a grip on her hand.

Pete was silent for a while. "I don't know. Just wondering, I guess." He hesitated. "Well, to tell you the truth I was thinking of asking Trini to go out with me, but since you and I are friends and everything, I thought I'd better ask."

Trini found her voice. "For God's sake, Pete, I'm sitting right here." She resisted the urge to snap the thick suspenders securely buttoned to his pants. The young man did have a small waist. Maybe he worried his pants would fall if he had to run.

Bobby snorted. She jabbed him in the ribs. Bobby jumped and cleared his throat. "I guess you can say we are," he said.

Trini felt a flush come to her cheeks. She hardly knew what to make of this. Did Bobby mean it? Or did he suspect how she felt about Pete and wanted to spare her his advances? Pete started talking again about baseball, but she tuned him out. She thought she heard a sound in the distance.

"Can you shut up for a second?" she whispered.

There it was again. A scraping sound. Like a foot dragging against the wood. Something was coming. Bobby shifted uneasily next to her.

Pete must have heard it, too. Before she could stop him, he was out the door, feet pounding away from them.

She turned to Bobby. "I told him we needed to stay together."

Bobby was on his feet, fumbling for his flashlight. "The guy's an idiot," he muttered.

He'd just flicked on the light, the beam swinging wildly against the walls, when they heard a scream. Pete. Definitely Pete. Coming from somewhere below.

On shaky legs, she followed Bobby out to the landing. The sounds of a scuffle followed by Pete's shrieks and a terrible deep throated grunting came from somewhere below. The temperature felt like it had dropped by ten degrees.

"We have to help him," Trini said, fighting a strong reluctance to move.

"Yeah," Bobby replied in a quiet voice. He turned off the flashlight, and they plunged into darkness.

Together, they moved down the steps, following the horrible racket. Trini focused on the noise, wandered too far to her right, plunged off the steps, and rolled down the dirt path until she hit a tree. She sat up, dazed.

Pete shouted again. This time, a desperate "Help me! Help me!"

His voice was much closer, coming from the far side of a shack to her left. Bobby ran up and pulled her to her feet. She patted her gun. It was still there in its holster. They skirted the tiny cabin.

She could see two figures struggling. Pete, on the ground, doing his best to fend off someone in a long, shapeless robe, whose outline she could make out from the glow of the streetlamps below.

"Leave him alone!" Bobby yelled.

The figure stopped and turned to face them.

Not too tall and strangely built, lumpy around the middle with arms far too long. A tangled mass of hair covered most of its face, except for a glimpse of sharp, jagged teeth and eyes that glittered red in the night. Then the figure hissed at them, and turned back to Pete, who was scrabbling backwards. Trini watched in horror as the creature grabbed Pete by his suspenders and dragged him away with astonishing speed.

"Jesus!" Bobby cried. His hand holding the flashlight was shaking.

As Pete whipped around a cabin, back scraping the hard ground, he grabbed a metal bucket as he shot past it. They could hear it clanging against rocks and steps along the steep path running next to a low rock wall. There was nothing to do but follow the sound.

"Trini! Bobby! For God's sake, help me!" shouted Pete.

They went after him. They found him further down the slope, half in, half out of a black space beneath a shack built into the side of a hill. An overhang propped up by two stilts. Pete gripped a wooden beam to keep himself from disappearing into the cavern. Trini remembered exploring it as a kid. Once. It had been too dark and creepy, even for her. The red-eyed figure was roaring in frustration as it tried to yank Pete inside by his suspenders.

If they didn't do something quick, Pete would slither into the black hole, and it would all be her fault because she'd invited him.

She remembered the switchblade he carried in his pocket. She'd have to act fast.

After a few quick words to Bobby, she dashed forward, dropped to her knees, and reached into Pete's pants' pocket; a task made more difficult because Pete was thrashing around, trying to dig his heels into the ground to keep from being dragged in. Finally, her fingers closed around the knife. With some difficulty, she opened it, then sawed at the closest suspender strap. When it snapped away from her like a living thing, she hacked away at the second one.

Pete was free. Bobby grabbed his legs and gave a mighty pull. Pete's head emerged from the dark space. His eyes were bulging, and his jaw was working. While Bobby yanked a dazed Pete away from the shack, Trini scrambled to her feet, dropping the knife and reaching for the gun. She took a step back as the lumpish figure stepped out of the gloom, its red eyes fixed on Trini.

She fired. To her great surprise, it dropped to the ground with an agonized howl. It crawled toward her.

Without waiting to see what else it was about to do, she stumbled toward Bobby and Pete. Together, they ran toward Palo Verde, Pete babbling. "Did you see it? Did you see its eyes? What was that? Because that was a monster, man. Like the Cucuy. Worse than the Cucuy! I swear it was going to eat me or something!"

Trini was so relieved Pete survived when they finally reached Bertita's house, she didn't even say, "I told you so, pendejo." Instead, she gave him a hug, collapsed onto the sofa and stared up at the ceiling until someone handed her a cold beer.

Chapter 13

Trini tried to follow Pete's ramblings, but a small hangover made that difficult.

She sat in the bright light of Bertita's kitchen, drinking coffee, still in the clothes she'd worn the night before. Bertita had insisted they let her sleep in. Rose had volunteered to cover for her at the store. Her father had woken early, she was told, and was taking a nap. There was no sign of Professor Miller or Lencha.

Bobby was staring at her with a concerned expression. His hair freshly washed and combed, he wore a white starched shirt and black pants. Even Pete had risen early, already dressed in his dusty work clothes.

Something he said caught her attention.

"What do you mean, you found blood?" she said.

Pete was pacing, a half-eaten pan dulce in his hands. "It's what I've been trying to tell you! I went back to the shacks this morning, as soon as it was light, and had a look around. I took some friends with me, don't worry." He paused long enough to give Trini a wistful look. "There was some blood on the ground where you shot it. The Cucuy thing. At least I think it was blood, but it was black instead of red. It left footprints in the dirt, so it wasn't a ghost or anything." He hesitated, frowning. "More like, you know. A monster."

Bertita was stirring a pot of beans simmering on the stove. "Ai, Pete, how many times do I have to tell you? They're demons!" she said over her shoulder.

"Okay, demons then," Pete replied. Leaning toward Trini, he gave her a conspiratorial wink. "Like it matters."

Trini stared at him. After everything they'd gone through, the guy was trying to be funny.

Before she could think of a response, he continued, "My friends saw some weirdos hanging around the top of Yolo Drive last night, hiding in the trees. They said they looked real spooky, their skin all white and stuff."

She stared into her cup of coffee, her mind racing to make sense of this latest information. "You still think they're from the Ku Klux Klan?"

Pete shook his head, serious. "No. No, I don't. Not after what Bertita said." Trini shot a glance at Bertita, who shrugged, then threw salt into the pot of beans.

"That's weird. I hit that thing, it bled, but no body," Trini said, more to herself than to anyone else in the room.

"That's what I said, like five times already," said Pete. "Well, my break is over. I gotta get back to work." He paused at the door. "Are we going back out tonight? Kick some more ass?"

Trini jumped up and gave him a shake. "Pete! Listen to me. You don't seem to understand. You almost got killed last night. You almost got *us* killed. I'm not sure what that was, but you are not going out looking for more trouble. Got it?"

Pete sighed, clicked his heels together and saluted. "Si, jefe," he said, then left.

She collapsed back into the chair and turned to Bobby. "I don't know what to think. About anything."

Bobby said, "I don't, either, but, after last night, seeing those red eyes up close? That was no mask. I think we need to talk to

82

Lencha. Find out what she knows because we haven't taken her seriously so far."

Bertita thumped her cane on the floor. When Trini glanced up, the old lady was pointing at her. "You'll listen to that young man if you know what's good for you, Trini Duran. The sooner you wise up, the better off we'll be because things are going to get worse around here." She banged out the side door. Seconds later, they could smell cigar smoke blowing in through the open window.

"She told you," Bobby said, a smile playing around his lips. "Should we talk to Lencha?"

Trini looked at Bobby in surprise. "Really, Mr. Community Organizer? You want to talk to the curandera? Guess what she's going to say? You heard Bertita. They think they're demons. We're going to get nothing but crazy talk."

Bobby rose from his chair, staring down at her, an odd expression on his handsome face. "Trini. Nothing can be any crazier than the last two nights. We can't keep denying what our own eyes have seen."

Trini felt something give way inside her. The last of her defenses against the unbelievable, she supposed.

There was no explanation for Dog-Face Bride, or the naked, hairy man, or the pale spooks that jumped as high as a house. The red-eyed creature that nabbed Pete had dragged him away as if he'd been a sack of potatoes. In two nights, she'd fired three shots at living things, not just tin cans. One might have hit its mark and done some damage, but the creep in the white dress and tattered veil should have dropped dead. Instead, the bullets went right through it.

It was time to stop fooling herself. Things were happening beyond anything she understood. In her world, if she studied for a multiple-choice test, she got a good grade. If she stocked the shelves right, customers were happy and bought things. If she practiced shooting tin cans, she could hit them.

She liked things that way. You tried and got results. The major reason she'd left Chavez Ravine. No matter how many letters she'd helped her father write to the city council, no matter how many times they'd gone to meetings to protest the eviction of thousands of people, the city people hadn't given a damn. All their efforts had come to nothing.

She'd stopped trying, gave up, and left, and now she was back in Palo Verde with events fast spinning out of control. And she didn't like it one bit.

"You're right," she said, pushing back from the table.

Bobby gave her a big smile as he helped her clear the plates. They found Lencha at the back of the property in a large shed she used to make her cures. A young woman scurried past them, clutching a jar to her chest. Her eyes were red from crying.

"A love potion," Lencha explained. "They don't work so good on married men," she added with a sigh. The curandera was wearing a yellow dress with a brown sweater and an apron made from a hundred-pound El Faro flour sack.

Trini was surprised to see Professor Miller sitting in a low chair in the corner, legs propped up on a wooden crate, a thin blanket over his knees, "I heard you had an eventful night," he said, peering over the top of his book. His blue eyes radiated concern.

"That's why we're here," Bobby said, looking around with open curiosity.

Morning light streamed in through the narrow gaps between the wooden slats. Rows of glass jars lined the tops of two workbenches. Dried herbs hung from the ceiling. Lencha ground something with a musky fragrance on a metate. Her brown hand rocked back and forth over the flat stone.

"Is that to keep the jumping men away from the house?" Trini asked.

Lencha shook her head. "I don't make that stuff in front of people," she said, then pressed her lips together.

Trini shot a glance at Bobby. This was going to be harder than they thought. Just because *they* had decided to talk to Lencha, it didn't mean the healer wanted to talk to them. Especially after how Trini had reacted to the notion of demons.

"I thought you could help us," said Bobby. "After last night."

Lencha turned her head away.

Professor Miller cleared his throat. "I'm sure Florencia will be happy to help you once you explain what you're after."

Trini gazed at him in astonishment. "Florencia!" she echoed. "Lencha's name is Florencia?" This was a new one on her. In all the years she lived in Chavez Ravine, not one person had ever mentioned it.

Lencha gave a tight-lipped smile as Professor Miller chuckled. "There's a lot you don't know about this woman."

Trini chanced a pleading look in his direction. If anyone could help sway Lencha, it was this man.

After a moment, he said. "Florencia, why don't you show them the little journal you showed me?"

Lencha sighed, then set the grinding stone on the bench and rummaged around on a tall shelf, standing on tiptoes. Her long black braid shot with silver strands hung down her back. Trini noticed with surprise she had a small, neat waist and well-shaped legs. It occurred to her the curandera wasn't as old as she'd thought. In the soft light of the shed, Lencha—or Florencia—looked beautiful. She handed a dog-eared notebook to Trini, who took it, suddenly filled with trepidation.

She sat on a skinny bench and opened it. Bobby joined her. It was a tight fit. He was so close she got a whiff of Lifebuoy soap. She hoped she didn't smell bad.

The first half of the journal was devoted to recipes for cures, made in a neat and steady hand. The penmanship impressed Trini. She wished she could write as pretty as that. Lencha leaned over them and tapped a folded piece of paper acting as a bookmark. Trini flicked it open to the right spot. They gazed at the notes.

Bobby looked up at Lencha. "You've been keeping track!"

"Someone had to," she muttered.

Whatever Trini had been expecting, it wasn't this. Lencha had recorded every strange sighting she'd heard about or seen herself, with dates, times, and descriptions.

Tuesday, September 13, Yolo Drive Loma at the top "Weirdos covered in white paint up to no good hanging around at night" - Rosie Baca

Wednesday, September 14 Bishop Road Palo Verde "Juan Martinez chased by an ugly man with horns when he was coming home at night with his fruit cart" - Alicia Rivera

Thursday, September 15, Brooks Avenue and Effie "An ugly, mean animal like a giant dog with no hair was sitting on the front porch of the Aguirre's house and wouldn't let them inside. I had to get my brother to come with a rifle, and the thing ran off." Manny Alvarado.

And on it went for pages, every entry stranger than the last, until she'd reached the entries documenting the attacks on her father, Hal, the professor and Pete. Trini's hands had gone sweaty. She wiped them on her soiled dungarees.

Bobby was rubbing the side of his face, eyebrows knit together in concentration. "The first date is September 13th," he said.

Lencha leaned against her worktable and crossed her arms in front of her chest. "A day of bad luck. Terrible luck."

"Is it?" Bobby said. "That's the day after the planning meeting where things got out of control. They didn't expect so many of us to show up. They called us agitators. Wouldn't let us inside. But there was this new reporter, the one I told you about, Trini, the one who's on our side. He started taking pictures and said if they didn't let us in, he'd write about it because we had a right to representation, and if they evicted anyone from the meeting before we brought it to a judge, he'd write about that, too. There were a few city guys who were mad about it. They're used to getting their way. Doing whatever they want to poor people and nobody caring, nobody challenging them. But they backed down. A couple of them are running for re-election, and they can't afford bad publicity."

"Are you saying they have something to do with what's going on here?" Trini asked, voice rising.

"I don't know, but it's got to be more than a coincidence."

Trini turned her attention to the curandera, who was now scraping a chunky yellow substance into a jar. "Lencha, why do you believe these weirdos are demons?"

Lencha shot her an exasperated look.

"Florencia," said Professor Miller. "You know not everyone believes in the spirit world."

Trini could not figure out Lencha. There they were, asking about the very thing she'd been trying to convince them of, and now she seemed reluctant to talk about it.

She went over to the woman and took both hands in hers. "Lencha, what is it? Please tell me because I don't understand."

Lencha looked her in the eyes. "I do a little magic I learned from my mother. She was a bruja."

Trini stepped back. Lencha's mother was a witch? Trini had never believed in the supernatural, but here was this woman talking about demons and witches. And Trini was listening because she didn't have any better explanation for what was going on.

Lencha continued. "My mother died before she could finish teaching me her ways. I don't have the powers she had, but I can do a few things to fight these demons. I can make some powders to keep them away, but I don't have the power to send them back where they came from."

Professor Miller cleared his throat. He held up a small book. Trini squinted at the title. "The Lost Art of Spirit Conjuring."

He said, "A friend brought this to me. Florencia is right. Someone is behind this, and from what Bobby says, it sounds to me like there's a witch somewhere who knows how to summon demons and send them to scare the people of Chavez Ravine. Or do more than scare us. Bobby, what do you know about the men on the city council?"

Bobby shot to his feet. "Those people?" he exclaimed. "A bunch of men in gray suits and wingtips? You're saying one of them is a witch?"

Professor Miller set down his book and regarded Bobby with piercing blue eyes. "Well, I don't expect our witch to show up wearing a funny hat and black cape. What he will have is motive. You're going to need to keep your eyes and ears open to see if you can figure out who it is."

Bobby threw up his hands. "And then what?"

"Then I can help you find out more about this person," Professor Miller said. "See what we're dealing with."

Trini and Bobby exchanged looks. The professor sounded so casual, like he was talking about the weather, not tracking down a witch who summons evil spirits.

"There's a planning committee meeting tonight," Bobby said.

Trini stuck her hands in her pockets, unable to believe what she was hearing. She felt powerless. How could they fight against things that defied the laws of nature?

She had two choices. She could walk away, return to Henry Loya's store and her nice little cottage, and ordered life. Or she could accept what Lencha and the professor were saying and learn how to confront whatever these things were.

"I'm coming with you to the meeting," Trini announced. She turned to Lencha. "Can you come too? You might be better at figuring out who is doing this than we are."

Spending the evening in a crowded meeting was safer than another night crouching in the darkness, watching out for boogeymen. But as she sat soaking in the clawfoot bathtub at home, she realized it wasn't all that different. Looking for something unfamiliar and scary. Except, this time, she'd have to leave her gun behind.

Chapter 14

Bobby hardly spoke on the drive to downtown Los Angeles. It took Trini a while to figure out what was bothering him. As it turned out, it had nothing to do with looking for a demon-conjuring witch. He was worried about the speech he was about to deliver.

"I'm the new community organizer," he said, pulling at his tie. "You went to those meetings last year, the ones that got rowdy?" When Trini nodded, he continued. "Then you heard the ladies speaking out against the housing project. Well, *they've* led the charge from the beginning, but they thought no one was listening because they're not only Mexican, they're Mexican *women*. So they brought me in."

Trini squirmed in her seat. "But you're still Mexican. And young. The ladies think they'll pay attention to you?"

Rose, behind the wheel, chuckled. "You've not heard this young man give a speech, Trini Duran. You've got quite a treat coming to you."

"We're supposed to be looking for a witch," she reminded everyone.

"*We* are," replied Rose. "Bobby's job tonight is to help us save our homes."

Bobby gave an enormous yawn. Then he tilted his head back. "God, I'm tired," he groaned, rubbing his face.

"If he can stay awake," Trini said, patting his shoulder.

Lencha had been silent on the ride to City Hall, although Trini couldn't help noticing her stiff shoulders and constant fidgeting.

Trini touched the herb-filled sachet she'd stuffed inside the sleeve of her sweater. Lencha had given a small pouch to everyone in the car, saying it would help protect them against any ill will. But less than ten minutes later, she'd admitted she wasn't sure it would work on a witch powerful enough to produce monstrous creatures.

Inside City Hall, Trini stepped through the double doors to the meeting room, surveying the scene. About a dozen people she recognized from Chavez Ravine stood at the back, carrying protest signs. Men in business suits clustered together at the front, talking. A narrow-faced woman in a black dress and white collar looked her up and down as she pushed past.

Trini was glad she'd taken extra trouble with her appearance. She'd chosen a square neck red dress with black piping and black heels. She'd even put her hair up in pin curls so it had a nice wavy style. But it was Bobby's reaction that mattered. When she'd walked out of the house, he'd done a double take.

"Trini! You look…" Then his voice had drifted off, and he flushed red. Trini had taken it as a compliment. Or surprised to see her in anything besides dungarees, with her hair combed for once.

Either way, she knew she could stand proudly, even surrounded by so many well-dressed strangers.

She took a deep breath and followed Rose's platinum bouffant across the shiny floor to the seats near the front Bobby saved for them. He was deep in conversation with a small man with chipmunk teeth.

Before they'd set out, Bobby explained it was a special committee meeting made up of a few elected officials, but mostly housing and planning bureaucrats to discuss what to do with the holdouts of Chavez Ravine. A problem, he said, they would rather solve behind closed doors. But several Mexican American groups had stepped in, demanding they open the meetings to the public, threatening protests. The committee had grudgingly agreed.

That reluctance was obvious by the sour expressions of the men seated around the curved wooden table facing the audience. Trini studied each of their faces. If there was a witch among them, he wasn't sprouting horns or carrying a wand. No obvious candidates. Yet.

When the clock struck seven, the chipmunk man called the meeting to order.

Another man with black hair like a shiny helmet leaned forward, elbows on the desk, and said, "Mr. Guerra. We're not sure why you are here tonight. Your presence is superfluous. Two-thirds of the Chavez Ravine residents have taken advantage of the opportunity given them and sold at top dollar to the City Housing Authority. If you had the interests of your people at heart, you'd be encouraging them to leave instead of filling their heads with pipe dreams."

Trini watched—muscles tensing—as Bobby rose to his feet, pulling his shoulders back, a vein twitching on his smooth bronze neck. "You're forgetting something, Mr. Dean," he began. "One-third of the residents still call Chavez Ravine home. Our community has been destroyed for nothing," Bobby paused, cleared his throat. "But it's not dead yet. You kicked out those families for a housing project that went up in smoke. So now what? Make the rest of them leave? Sell up for less than their properties are worth, like the rest did? Why should they go? For what? There are no plans for the land. You tricked most of the people into leaving, but the resisters won't fall for it."

Cheers went up at the back of the room. Bobby waved a sheaf of papers over his head. "I'd like to submit written testimony of more than a dozen residents forced to sell their homes in Palo Verde, La Loma and Bishop and move elsewhere. They've learned they're not free to buy another home wherever they want, and sometimes, they're not accepted in their new communities. We must prevent the same thing happening to the remaining residents. It would be cruel to uproot them only to experience this same heartbreak."

Trini felt her heart swell. Rose was right. Bobby was more than a smooth talker.

She glanced around, trying to gauge the reaction in the room, when she spotted Weechie across the aisle. All decked out, hands pressed to her heart, mouth open. What was *she* doing here? Weechie had never shown any interest in the movement to save Chavez Ravine. Bobby must have mentioned the meeting. Weechie turned and waved. Trini forced a smile to her lips, then dragged her eyes back to the helmet-haired man. "Housing" read his nameplate.

"And let it become a slum again?" Mr. Dean scoffed. "Because that's what it was, Mr. Guerra. Take off those rose-colored lenses. We discussed the deplorable housing conditions at a meeting two months ago, if you'll remember. Surveys showed two-thirds of the so-called houses up there used substandard materials. One-third didn't even have toilets. And the roads up there! A disgrace."

"And who is to blame for that?" Bobby thundered. "The city refused request after request to grade the dirt roads. Along with refusing to do anything about putting in drainage and streetlights. La Loma has one streetlight. One! Instead of deciding to tear down all those substandard houses as you call them, you could have forced the landlords to fix them up and bring them up to code. Instead, you voted to tear it all down without hearing from the residents. These hard-working people, these taxpayers, these American citizens never got a chance to say what they wanted."

Cheers from the back of the room. Bobby continued, "Mr. Dean, please tell us. What is your plan? You can't say because you don't have one. Until you do, you have no rightful claim to force these people out." Mr. Dean gave a dismissive sniff.

Another man, with a round red face and yellow hair, raised his hand. "I'd like to chime in here." When Mr. Dean nodded, he said, "You realize, don't you, Mr. Guerra, you are at odds with your fellow Mexican activists? The ones who endorsed public housing as part of their social agenda. I don't see any of them here tonight. And I will remind you the area in question, Mr. Guerra, is key to plans for downtown Los Angeles. In clearing that slum and re-directing the residents to more sanitary housing, we are accomplishing not one but two worthwhile goals for all our citizens and the betterment of our community."

A round of applause went up. Trini wanted to punch him. Hearing him describe her home as a slum was just too much.

Rose leaned over Lencha and poked Trini's arm. "Bigots," she muttered.

Bobby was opening his mouth to reply when Trini kicked the back of his foot. Startled, he gazed down at her as if surprised to see her there. She crooked a finger, and he bent down in response. "Tell them you know they're up to something to make people leave," she whispered into his ear.

Bobby straightened up and faced the sour-faced officials. "Gentlemen, there's another matter I'd like to raise. The residents report strangers are coming into Chavez Ravine at night trying to scare them. Does anyone know anything about that?"

The audience gasped. Camera flashes began going off.

Trini watched the reactions of the men at the table. Most looked surprised—except for the man on the far left, staring at Bobby through narrowed eyes. She nudged Lencha, but when she glanced down at her companion, the woman was trembling. Her shoulders were rising and falling under her brown coat, eyes locked on the man. Trini followed her gaze. The man didn't look scary. More like a professor than anything. Receding silver hair. Bushy black eyebrows. Dark mustache. White beard. Thick black glasses. But the way he fixed on Bobby was creepy. Trini felt a shiver run down her spine.

Trini paid little attention to what happened during the rest of the meeting. When it was over, they had decided nothing. Someone said something about doing another study. More limbo for the holdouts.

Rose, noticing Lencha's gray face, whisked her off to the bathroom.

Weechie rushed over to Bobby and made a big fuss, throwing her arms around him and congratulating him on making such a fine speech. Trini sat there, seething. Weechie blew her a kiss before sauntering off, hips swinging.

A young man approached, a camera hanging from a strap around his neck. A reporter, she guessed. Bobby introduced him as Mel Hayder. Trini gave a polite nod.

"I've heard you've made Councilman Tuck very unhappy," Mel said to Bobby.

"Oh, yeah?" Bobby said, lifting his eyebrows.

"My sources say he's pushing to clear the neighborhoods, but not everyone is on board. There are some crazy rumors going around. I hear he's talking with powerful people who have plans for the ravine. Big plans."

Bobby frowned. "What kind of plans?"

"No idea," said Mel, shrugging. "I'm having a hard time getting people to talk on the record. Tuck makes people nervous. But I'll tell you one thing. When the last of the holdouts leave, he wants to keep it quiet. He doesn't want it hitting the newspapers and everyone making a big deal over it."

Bobby chuckled. "Well, that's not going to happen. He sent a guy to talk to me to see if we could work something out, and I said no. We need every advantage we can get, and that includes making sure people know what Tuck is up to."

Trini recrossed her legs, blinking. Bobby had failed to mention any involvement with the man.

Mel snorted. "Yeah, he sent one of his goons to my editor, too. He offered an exclusive in exchange for us backing off covering Chavez Ravine. My editor told him to fuck off. If you want my advice, Bobby, watch your back."

Then he hurried off, leaving Trini to stare at Bobby in disbelief.

"You didn't tell me Tuck sent one of his people to talk to you," she whispered as he led her out of the room.

"It's nothing new. Hardball politics, that's all," he replied.

When they entered the main hall, Rose and an ashen-faced Lencha were waiting for them.

"I know who it is," Lencha said faintly. "The one with the white beard. The Tuck man."

Chapter 15

Rose was driving past Duran Market & Liquor when Bobby shouted, "Stop!" Rose slammed on the brakes, throwing everyone forward.

Bobby clawed at the door handle, leapt out of the car, and ran toward the former liquor store he rented from her father.

Trini stared after him, panicked. It was ten o'clock and dark out. On the drive into Palo Verde, they'd seen no signs of the boogeymen, but that didn't mean they weren't out there, waiting and hiding.

"Bobby!" she cried, scrambling out of the backseat. "What the hell do you think you're doing?"

Bobby had made it up the steps leading to the empty storefront next to the grocery. He was fumbling in his pocket for his keys. She hurried up the steps, slowed down by her heels.

"There's someone inside," he said over his shoulder.

She needed him to stop a moment, think. There was no time to be polite. She hauled off and slugged his arm.

"Ow!" he protested.

"Slow down, Bobby," she said, peering through the window of the empty room. He was right. Someone—or something—was in there, a strange light bobbing around inside. "I don't have my gun, and you don't have your bat," she reminded him. "There's no telling what's in there."

Lencha appeared at her side. On her soft, flat shoes, she'd managed not to make a sound as she approached. She shoved something into Trini's hands. A wooden baton.

"Rose told me to give this to you," Lencha whispered. "She carries it under her seat for protection." It felt heavy in Trini's hands. The thing was so sturdy she could imagine it breaking bones or smashing heads. Trini tried to picture Rose using it, and she could. Easily.

Bobby snatched it away, giving Lencha an exasperated look. "I'll take that," he snapped. "You two stay out here. Whoever is inside is probably after some of my papers. Opposition research."

Before they could reply, Bobby was sticking the key into the lock.

Lencha tapped Trini's elbow and said, "Rose went to get Pete."

Trini felt a rush of relief. Pete was down the street, keeping watch at Bertita's while they were away. It wouldn't take long for him to arrive. But she wasn't about to let Bobby go inside, alone, and she didn't have a weapon. Then she thought of her shoes. They had metal caps on the end of each heel. If she swung one hard enough, it would leave a nice dent. She slipped her shoes off and grabbed Bobby by the back of his jacket to keep him from going in without her.

The key appeared to be stuck. No amount of shaking the handle would open the door. "We'll have to go through the apartment," Bobby said.

Trini hurried after him down the narrow, dark path between the two buildings.

This time, the key worked. Bobby flicked on the light, holding the baton like a baseball bat. Trini surveyed the place, alert for danger. Nothing out of place. Nothing jumped out at them. A faint red light was coming in through the crack beneath the door to the outer room, but she couldn't hear anything.

"Bobby, remember what the reporter said? To watch your back. That Tuck guy could have sent someone, and you—we—will walk right into it."

"That I can deal with," he replied, then pushed open the connecting door.

A red, pulsating glow filled the long room. Except for the long table and chairs, it was empty. Nowhere to hide, not even a closet. Trini relaxed a bit. So did Bobby, letting the baton drop to his side. The light had to be coming from somewhere. She moved forward, her eyes scanning the room, under the chairs and table, covered with neat stacks of paper. Nothing.

Once her eyes had adjusted to the strange light, she spotted a glowing white cloud hovering over the papers. She blinked, her gaze following the dense mist upward to the ceiling. A red ball of light hovered in the air, just below the ceiling. A black spot in the middle, surrounded by a swirl of white and red vapors. She froze, a strange feeling washing over her. She didn't know what it was, but it looked dangerous. It perched there, waiting. Waiting for something. She backed away.

The papers on the desk curled and blackened as if burned by an invisible flame.

Bobby walked toward the table, as if in a trance.

"Don't, Bobby!" she said. "Stay back. It's too dangerous!"

Bobby ignored her. She rushed forward, grabbed him by the arm, and yanked so hard he stumbled backward.

Chaos broke out behind them, people and noise filling the room. Heavy footsteps and shouts. Pete Chavira and some guys she recognized as thugs from the neighborhood. They came to an abrupt stop as they spotted the light, eyes bulging.

"No one do anything," Trini warned, spreading her arms wide as if that were enough to keep everyone back.

"Don't get near it," Lencha shouted. "It can burn you. Or kill you."

"What is it?" Trini asked, voice shaking. The light was flickering, menacing. It cast strange shadows on the faces of Pete and his companions.

"La Luz Mala," said Lencha, sounding awestruck. "The bad light. My mother used to tell me about it." She made a hasty sign of the cross, and Trini could hear her murmuring a prayer.

The papers on the desk began to disintegrate. Trini heard Bobby give an agonized moan.

"Fuck that shit," bellowed Pete. Then he shoved them aside and grabbed the baton from Bobby's hand.

Trini watched in horror as Pete hopped onto a chair and prepared to take a swing.

"Ai, no, Pete!" Lencha cried. "Don't do it!"

"It's not a piñata, pendejo!" Trini shrieked, which she immediately regretted because Pete's buddies snapped out of their stupor.

They cheered him on. Trini wished Pete wore a blindfold, like the game of piñata, because then the idiot might miss. But by his expert stance, there was not much chance of that happening.

Pete swung. The baton connected with the ball of light, and for a second, nothing happened. Then it exploded in a blinding burst of white, and Pete screamed. He tumbled off the chair, writhing on the ground. Pete's friends stared at him, too shocked to move. Lencha and Bobby were frozen, too.

Pete lay convulsing under the light ball in the path of the mist. A noxious stench filled the air, making everyone cough. The acrid odor reminded Trini of the time a skunk sprayed their old dog, but worse.

Trini was the first to move. "Someone open the door!" she yelled. "We need some fresh air in here."

She was less worried about what might be outside than what the fumes might do to them. Bobby bolted toward the door and flung it open. The cool night air wafted in.

Turning her attention to Pete's friends, she yelled, "Help me get him away from that thing!"

She grabbed Pete's legs; then, his buddies sprang into action. Together, they dragged him into Bobby's kitchen. Bobby slammed the door behind them as Lencha bent over Pete, taking stock of his injuries as he stared up at the ceiling, whimpering. Angry red welts bubbled up over his face and neck. Lencha made soothing, clucking sounds with her tongue as she poked and prodded, assessing the damage.

Bobby wet dish towels and stuffed them into the crack of the door to keep the fumes from coming in. Trini crouched next to Lencha. Pete's eyes bulged with pain and fear. But when they met hers, they were alert. Trini hoped it was a good sign.

"Is he going to be okay?" she whispered.

"I'm not sure," Lencha replied, then crossed herself.

Chapter 16

Trini checked on Pete early the next morning. Still covered in painful red welts, he grimaced with every movement and whimpered in his sleep. He'd refused to go to the hospital, so Rose and Martin had driven to Chinatown to fetch Dr. Eng. The doctor said if they hadn't dragged him away from the poisonous vapor as quickly as they did, it might have ruined his lungs and killed him. Dr. Eng didn't seem to doubt the story of "the bad light" but accepted it as part of the strange goings-on.

Trini crept away on wobbly legs, relieved Pete had survived. The guy was an impetuous pendejo, but he had a big heart. When asked to come to their aid, he hadn't hesitated.

Her head still throbbed from whatever nasty stuff the ball of light released, and she was still coughing. Her favorite red dress and Bobby's white shirt and black pants hung outside on the clothesline to dry. She'd washed them in the steel tub on Bertita's back porch, to scrub away the stink.

Bertita's big house was filling up fast with victims of whatever the hell was going on in Chavez Ravine. First, her father, then the professor, and now, Pete. Good thing Bertita had enough rooms for everyone.

Trini had slept on the couch with Bobby passed out on the floor next to her. When the sun rose, they'd walked up the road to his place, unsure what they might find.

The front door was still wide open. The ball of light—or La Luz Mala, as Lencha called it—had disappeared. So had the papers Bobby worried about all night. Only scraps and ashes remained. It had taken Bobby months to gather the documents and testimonies proving Chavez Ravine wasn't a slum, no matter what the city officials said. In fact, it was no worse than other parts of Los Angeles. The real problem had more to do with the lack of political power of its residents.

They returned to the big house for coffee in Bertita's bright kitchen.

"It's always about land in this city," the professor said, sounding disgusted. "Wealthy folks and city officials love talking about blight and slums and how their renewal projects will fix all that. When it comes down to it, the regular people are pushed out, and up goes some project that benefits private developers."

Trini shot him an appreciative glance. The professor knew a lot more than just writing and history. She turned to Bobby and said, "You heard what the reporter guy Mel said. Councilman Tuck is making plans for the ravine, except nobody knows what they are. That's why he's in such a hurry to make us leave."

Bobby's eyebrows shot up. "You said we again."

"Yes," Trini said, tipping back in her chair. She wished she was wearing something other than a borrowed housedress in faded pink, but at least it was clean. "Yes, Bobby, I did. I've lived most of my life in Palo Verde, remember? I may not win any community organizer awards, but I'm here, aren't I?" Her father cleared his throat from where he stood leaning against the doorframe. When she glanced over at him, he was grinning. She returned his smile and continued. "What the hell are we going to do? Like you said last night, they killed the housing project. The city's got no plans for this place—"

"That they will admit," interrupted Bobby.

"That they will admit," Trini conceded, feeling her father come up behind her and place his hands on her shoulders. "But someone is trying to scare us off," she continued, voice rising. "And we're almost sure those freaks we're seeing aren't hired goons. You saw Lencha's reaction to Councilman Tuck, but you didn't see how he was watching you, Bobby. Like looks could kill. Then, a couple of hours after you let 'em know the people aren't backing down, some evil light ball appears and destroys your papers. That is no coincidence."

The side door was open. Bertita sat on a stool outside the door, smoking a cigar. "The girl's right," she said. "That was no coincidence."

Salvio Duran limped toward a vacant chair, wearing a plaid bathrobe. His leg was still giving him trouble. Unlike the professor, he looked worn and tired with dark circles under his eyes. At least he was out of bed and upright, Trini thought. Dr. Eng had warned her a full recovery could take months.

Restless, she got up and began pacing. Bobby was lost in his own thoughts, still wearing the gloomy expression that had taken hold of his handsome features.

She wasn't sure why she was feeling so riled up. It's not as if anyone in the room disagreed with her. They were on the same side, but her mind was all over the place, her thoughts scattered like dry leaves after a windstorm. She halted, biting her lip as she thought things over.

If damn Councilman Tuck had a plan, they needed one too. More than sitting around in a dark attic, waiting. Lencha believed Tuck was a powerful witch. That needed figuring out, too.

Folding her arms across her chest, she said, "How do we find out more about Tuck? I want to make sure we're not imagining things." Lencha shot her a dirty look, offended Trini questioned her judgment. Trini added, "Sorry, Lencha. I know you're right, but we need some proof."

Lencha nodded.

The professor shoved back from the table and got to his feet. All cleaned up and rested, he looked younger than she'd first thought.

"That's something I can look into," he said, blue eyes twinkling with enthusiasm. "I have some old friends downtown I haven't seen in a while. They might know a thing or two."

Lencha placed a hand on his arm. "If you hurry, Rose can give you a ride downtown. She hasn't left yet." The professor pecked her cheek and left. Everyone stared. Lencha blushed and began bustling around, fixing Salvio something to eat.

Trini resumed her pacing. There was still something nagging at her. "I still don't get why I missed Dog-Face Bride when I shot at her. We were a couple yards away. But I shot the red-eyed Cucuy, and I could hardly see a thing because it was so dark. My bullets went right through one but hit the other. So, what's the difference?"

Bobby lifted his head, frowning. "Well, what if they are different kinds of monsters?"

Trini did a double take. She couldn't remember him using the word before.

"Demons," said Lencha, setting a rolled-up tortilla in front of Salvio. Menudo simmered on the stove. Salvio looked up at her with gratitude, but also with sadness.

"I'm sorry to be such a bother," he said. Lencha shook her head and squeezed his shoulder.

Trini stopped in front of Bobby and stared down at him. She ran a hand over her hair. She was sure it was a wild mess, and she'd forgotten to braid it. "Different how?"

Bobby shrugged. "What if one is a ghost, and you *can't* shoot it. And the other is a monster, so you *can* shoot it or stab it or whatever."

"I think he's onto something," Salvio said, inspecting his tortilla to make sure it had enough butter.

Trini was silent for a while. She retied the cloth belt of her housedress. The darn thing kept coming undone. Then she poured herself another cup of coffee and sat across from Bobby, staring into his brown eyes. In the soft morning light, she noticed they had tiny flecks of gold.

She cleared her throat. "That's another problem we need to solve. What, exactly, are we dealing with?"

This, at least, was familiar territory. Taking stock was something she knew how to do. But this would be more dangerous than walking around Duran Market & Liquor with a clipboard.

Bobby coughed. "What did you have in mind? I'm not sure I can take another exciting night with you, Trini."

At this, Salvio's eyes snapped open. Trini kicked Bobby under the table. He grimaced and bent over to rub his shin. "I'm just teasing your daughter, Mr. Duran," Bobby said, registering Trini's stricken expression.

Trini leaned forward, locking eyes with Bobby to make sure she had his full attention.

He rubbed his forehead as if he had a headache coming on. "What? What do you want to do now?"

"We need to take inventory," she announced. "Tonight. If we're going to fight these things and try to keep Chavez Ravine."

Chapter 17

Slingshots made the most sense, Trini concluded. They couldn't go around firing guns at every freak they saw. And what Pete's buddies—Ruben, Tony, Richard, and Junie—lacked in the brains department, they more than made up for it in aim and a desire for revenge.

"Whatever you want to do, Trini, you let us know," said Ruben, thumping his chest three times. "They're gonna be sorry they messed with Pete."

They didn't seem as worried about demons and monsters as they should be, something Trini put down to spending too much time in juvie and one too many knocks on the head at the boxing gym. But they'd spent plenty of time working on their slingshot skills, which they showed off with great theatricality. She had to admit they were pretty damn good.

Bobby couldn't hit the side of a tree.

"That's okay," she said, watching his shots go wide. "Someone needs to take the inventory." She was back to wearing her dungarees, boots, and braided hair. Bobby made a face, reached out and pulled one of her braids.

"Ouch, Bobby," she protested, rubbing her scalp. "I'm tender headed."

"Could have fooled me," he scoffed.

Ruben watched this exchange with interest. Later, when he and Trini had a moment alone together, he'd said, "He's flirting with you," which made her heart swell.

Not that she considered Ruben a romance expert. His idea of flirting involved whistling at girls and making rude noises. Still, it made her wonder how Bobby felt about her. Sometimes, she caught him looking at her in a funny way. She hoped one of these days he'd get around to kissing her, but doubted it would happen anytime soon, not with everyone hanging around all the time.

As the afternoon wore on, Pete's buddies began showing signs of the jitters. They'd taken to arguing over what kind of ammunition to use—steel balls, lead balls, marbles, or rocks.

Trini stepped in and said, "I don't much care as long as you stay hidden, where you're supposed to. The first pinche who pulls a Pete is gonna get shot in the nalgas. By me."

They agreed to spread out in pairs over La Loma and Palo Verde in the spots where Lencha had documented boogeyman sightings. Bishop had been spared the strange visitations. Bobby said this made sense since so many people in the neighborhood had sold up to the city. It made Trini nervous to have the guys out on their own where she couldn't monitor them but, there was no way around it. She'd have to trust them.

Her father had presented her with a pendant of El Santo Nino de Atocha on a silver chain to help protect her. The professor had bought it from a stall outside La Placita Church with the money Salvio had given him and had taken it to a priest for a special blessing. The unexpected gift had brought tears to Trini's eyes.

The first night on patrol, they didn't see a thing. Not one of the pasty-faced jumpers. Not the short naked hairy man. Not Dog-Face Bride or the red-eyed Cucuy she'd shot at the shacks in Loma.

"I guess even spooks need a night off," Bobby grumbled as they walked through the moonlight back to Bertita's house.

While they didn't catch any monsters, things had gone better than she could have hoped. Only two mishaps. Tony fell out of a tree and suffered bumps and bruises, and Richard got shot in the ass with a BB. Later, they admitted it happened while goofing around.

The next afternoon, she accompanied Bobby to Bishop and watched a bulldozer plow through a clapboard house until it collapsed, leaving the roof sitting on top of a pile of sticks and rubble. Trini couldn't bear to watch anymore; it was too depressing. Bishop was the smallest village in Chavez Ravine. It looked like a ghost town. Empty spots where houses once stood. A few men scavenged for bricks, windows, and doors, loading them into a truck.

Bobby must have noticed her grim expression because he slung an arm over her shoulder. "It's not too late, you know," he said. "We still might save the other neighborhoods."

He held her hand all the way back to Palo Verde. They stopped in front of the market, where customers waited for her to open.

"I'll pick you up at six, and we can go to Bertita's," he said, like they had a date. She stared after him, wondering how it was possible to miss someone the moment they said goodbye.

Bertita and Lencha had spent the day making tamales. Trini contributed by bringing vanilla ice cream from the market. Martin and Rose arrived loaded down with bottles of red wine. Pete had recovered enough to join them for the evening meal, although Lencha kept reminding him not to scratch the welts, covered in a cream she'd concocted.

When everyone had settled in at the long table, the professor cleared his throat. "I have some information about Councilman Tuck."

Trini's mouth went dry. She took a sip of red wine and waited for the professor to continue.

He said, "As Bobby knows, Spencer Tuck is at the end of his first term, facing re-election. Things aren't looking too good for the man because he hasn't endeared himself to his constituents."

Martin poured the professor a glass of wine. He was reaching for it when Lencha whisked it away. The professor gazed wistfully at the bottle as Martin topped up Rose's glass.

Bertita thumped her cane on the floor. "You mean the voters?" she asked. Lencha shot her a dark look. Bertita shrugged. "Why use a long word when a short one works just fine?" she grumbled.

"As Bobby also knows," the professor continued, "this was Tuck's first job as an elected official. Or in government, for that matter. He ran as an outsider with big ideas. Most people know him because he's a novelist. A popular one. And a scholar—"

"But is he a witch?" Trini interrupted.

The professor gave a short laugh. "You were always to the point, Trini. You used to bring me your assignments when you were a little girl full of questions. Why didn't the teacher let you do a book report on Annie Oakley? Why did the teacher give you a B instead of an A? Questions I couldn't answer, at least, not honestly. Now I have an answer for you."

"And?" Trini pressed, dark eyes never leaving his face.

Professor Miller gave a heavy sigh. "Yes. He's a witch, and a devious one, it seems. He claims he's made a study of magic and the occult, and that's all. But I hear he's a hereditary witch who can trace his magical ancestry to Seventeenth Century, Ireland. And some people believe he invented a magical system of rituals and symbols that allows him to command evil spirits to do his bidding."

The table erupted in gasps and murmurs.

Bobby looked stunned. "But he's a councilman! Who told you all this?"

The professor returned Bobby's stare. "There are important people who know things. People willing to talk because we've known each other a long time, and they trust me to keep their secrets. I'm sorry young man, but I can't reveal my sources."

For Trini, the meaning sunk in all at once. She studied the tamale on her plate. All this talk of witches had made her lose her appetite.

Trini regarded the professor through narrowed eyes. "Do you believe it? That he's a witch?" she demanded, voice rising.

The professor shrugged. "Would it matter if I did?" He put a large hand over Lencha's dainty, brown one. "This wonderful woman believes it with her heart and soul. And I believe her. But more importantly, Tuck believes it, and so do his followers."

Salvio lurched to his feet. "But what does a witch want with Chavez Ravine?" he asked. His voice shook with indignation. "This is a dusty kind of place. It's no Beverly Hills or Santa Monica."

"It's the land, Daddy," Trini said. "That's what Bobby's been saying all along. Without all the houses and so close to downtown, the land is even more valuable." She watched as her father sank back into his chair, looking gray and deflated.

Bobby nodded absently. Shifting in his chair he said, "This magical system you were talking about. If we could find out more, is it something we could use against him?" Trini liked the sound of that. But they'd need more serious ammunition than rocks and BB's.

The professor relaxed into a smile. "That's an excellent idea, young man. I'll see what I can find out first thing tomorrow morning." Then he dug into his tamale.

Chapter 18

By ten o'clock, everyone was in position, hiding somewhere in Palo Verde or La Loma, slingshots in hand. Pete's buddies chose their hiding places well, in trees or on roofs overlooking paths leading into the neighborhoods. The moon and the stars were especially bright, the air cold and still. Bundled up in a well-worn hunting jacket, Trini crouched next to Bobby, wearing a long coat that made him look like a Zoot Suiter. Both had belonged to Bertita's husband.

They'd chosen a narrow alley between two empty houses at the top of a hill with a view of Elysian Park in the distance. A steep staircase separated them from the road. Bobby had found a large piece of plywood to cover the entrance to the alley, leaving enough space for them to monitor the street below.

Trini's heart thudded in her chest. She hated all the waiting, and there was so much that could go wrong. She had her gun, just in case, and Bobby had brought Rose's wooden baton.

Time passed slowly. Trini checked her watch, using the flashlight under her jacket to see the time. A quarter to twelve. Her eyes had finally adjusted to the darkness.

"I see something," Bobby whispered.

A group of tall, pale figures emerged from the trees at the top of the road. Walking together, long arms hanging down at their sides, they steadily approached. Four of them. From Trini's vantage point, it was impossible to see their faces. The skin of their legs looked impossibly pale under their hooded robes. Their footsteps made no sounds. How could she have ever thought they were people, circus freaks or thugs hired to scare them?

"Here they come," Bobby whispered.

Still, she hesitated. She had a straight line of sight. There were enough of them she would surely hit one, but she might as well wave a red flag over her head and yell, "Woo-hoo, here we are!"

"Get ready to run," she said.

She leaned forward and took aim. The lead ball whizzed through the air and went straight through one of the pale creatures in the middle of the pack. The hooded figure continued on its way as if nothing had happened. And maybe it hadn't.

"Did I miss?" she croaked.

Bobby continued to peer through the gap. "No. No way. Try it again."

"I can't believe this is happening," Trini muttered as she loaded another lead ball into the sling.

This time, she targeted the straggler of the group, smaller than the rest. She held the frame horizontally, parallel to the ground, drew back, aimed, and fired. The pale figure was oblivious to the lead ball passing through it.

Trini swallowed, shoving the slingshot into a pocket. "I guess that means it's a ghost. Now what?"

Bobby sighed. "Wait some more and see if anything else turns up." He took out a small notebook and scribbled something inside, then slipped it back into his pocket.

"I wonder how the guys are doing?" she said. Then both fell silent, eyes scanning the countless places where more strange creatures could appear.

Another fifteen minutes passed.

"See there?"

Holding the binoculars to his eyes with one hand, Bobby pointed with his free hand at the trees at the top of the road.

She saw it. And heard it, too, in the stillness of the night. Branches rustling and a crunching as something moved over the dried leaves on the ground.

It appeared at the top of the road. Trini gasped as it loped closer to them.

She'd never seen an uglier thing on four legs. Taller and bigger than a dog, but skinnier, too. Nearly bald, with patches of long straggly hair. Its head resembled a horned pig. Even from a distance, Trini could smell it, like something rotting. It halted on the road directly below them. Lifting its head, it sniffed the air. She pulled the slingshot from her pocket.

"Use your gun," Bobby whispered.

Trini shook her head. She would have liked nothing more than to shoot the thing dead, but she didn't want to risk the noise bringing other creatures their way, and besides, what if it were a ghost animal? She pushed herself to her feet and got into position.

The animal spotted her immediately, an ominous growl coming from its twisted mouth. Trini aimed at its head and let the sling go. She heard Bobby's swift intake of breath as the beast staggered and yelped. The thing was no ghost.

"Oh, Fudge," she muttered, watching as it pawed the ground like a bull and lurched toward them, leaving her no options.

She dropped the slingshot and grabbed the gun from its holster, firing as the foul-smelling monster leapt up the steps toward them. The shot found its target. The beast toppled over.

They crept out of their hiding place and slowly approached the body. Holding the baton over his head, Bobby prodded it with the toe of his boot. No movement.

"It's dead," Bobby said, then loudly exhaled.

Trini stared down at the thing she'd killed, a quickening in her chest. It was no ordinary animal—its body covered with thick, wrinkled skin. A new, even worse stench rose from the hole she'd blown in its chest.

"We better get out of here," she said, stepping past it.

When Trini and Bobby made it to the meeting place at the bottom of Brooks Avenue in Loma, they found the guys already gathered there, leaning against a fence, smoking cigarettes. Trini let out a tremendous sigh of relief. Everyone was there, thank God. All six of them. No one was bleeding.

Trini put a shaky hand to her head. "Well? What happened?"

"There were so many of those fuckers I ran out of ammo," Ruben replied, flicking a cigarette butt.

Tony snorted. "Only because you can't shoot worth a shit."

Ruben gave Tony a hard push, sending him stumbling. "They went straight through, pendejo."

"We shot at a bunch of ghosts," said Richard, sounding disappointed. "They didn't even do anything."

A guy named Frank snickered. "Not us, man. We nailed a hairy son of a bitch pretty good. He was totally naked. I'm pretty sure I got him in the cojones. You should have heard him scream."

"Yeah," said a guy with sleepy, hooded eyes. "There was this thing that looked like the Cucuy, I swear. Red eyes and everything. I got him with my slingshot, but that made him mad, so he came after me."

Bobby sidled up next to her. "That's Junie," he whispered into her ear. "Knifed a guy a couple of months ago." This did not surprise Trini. Pete Chavira, she knew, hung around with a rough crowd. But, on a night like tonight, this wasn't a bad thing as long as they were on the same side.

"And then, what happened?" she asked, resting her hands on her slender hips.

"I stabbed him," Junie announced calmly. "Made him bleed real bad, but he crawled away into some bushes." His lips curled into a grin. "We didn't go after him, though. Didn't think you'd like that."

Trini lifted her eyebrows. "You're right." She hesitated. "But I'm glad you're okay, Junie. Thank you."

Junie blinked. "Yeah, sure, Trini. Anytime."

Trini's attention wandered off to a straggly row of mailboxes nailed to wooden posts. Almost everyone on Brooks Avenue had sold up and left, except for Lencha, who still owned a small house on the block. But she wasn't thinking about the families or where they'd gone. Instead, she'd been focused on the inventory they'd set out to collect.

"Bobby," she said. "Remember when I hit the red-eyed thing that tried to take Pete? What time was that?"

"A few minutes after midnight," he answered firmly. "I know because I checked."

"And the rest of the times I shot but missed. Do you think that was before midnight?"

Bobby frowned and scratched his chin. "Yeah. Closer to eleven, I'd guess."

"I looked at my watch when those white jumpy things walked by us. It was quarter to twelve. It had to be around midnight when the monster pig showed up. Right?"

"Right, or a little after," Bobby said, eyes widening.

"What if before midnight, those things are ghosts? Or demons or whatever. We can try to hurt them, but we can't. But after midnight, they change. They become," Trini paused, searching for the right word. "More real. And then we can hurt them, kill them, like regular people. Or animals."

Bobby snatched his flashlight from his pocket. Shining it on his wristwatch, he said, "It's quarter to one. If what you said is right, we need to find out how long they stay real. Is it after midnight to dawn or whatever? Or just for a while?"

Trini regarded him for a moment, then kissed his cheek. "That's exactly what we need to do," she said, bounding back to the group to order them back into position.

An hour later, they had their answer. More strange figures and creatures appeared. But every pellet, rock, and marble passed straight through them.

Chapter 19

As best they could figure, the creatures were vulnerable to attack between midnight and one in the morning.

Ruben and his buddies searched La Loma and Palo Verde at dawn, and reported they'd found no evidence of the monsters they'd encountered overnight except for a few trails of what appeared to be blackish blood.

Weechie stumbled into the market minutes after it opened, wild-eyed and out of breath.

Trini couldn't remember ever seeing her friend so upset. Without all her makeup and red lipstick, she looked younger than her twenty-three years. Sagging against the counter, she held up both hands covered in red scratches, a crusty-looking bandage covering the knuckles of her right hand.

"What happened to you?" Trini gasped. She pulled up a chair with a back and settled her friend into it.

Weechie sniffed, eyes pooling with tears. "You won't believe me. Is Bobby around? I should tell him, too."

A flicker of exasperation crossed Trini's face. Even in the state she was in, Weechie didn't miss a trick. Trini said nothing and went to fetch Bobby from next door. Weechie held out her shaking hands. Trini wondered if this was an added touch of drama for Bobby's sake, and then felt guilty for having such uncharitable thoughts about her injured friend.

"It's okay," Trini said, patting Weechie's shoulder. "You can tell us now."

Weechie swallowed. "After the meeting last night, I met some friends. We went dancing, and we stayed later than we meant to because the music was so good. I got a ride, but not all the way home. I had to walk up the hill all the way to my house. It was dark, and I was all by myself, and then I heard this awful noise in the sky. There were these birds. Huge ones." She hesitated, staring down at her pitiful hands. "Here's the weird part. The birds had giant wings, but like bats, and they had teeth. I started running, and they came after me, going after my head. I put my hands up, and that's how they got all messed up. My brothers heard me screaming, and some neighbors did, too. They had to use bats and sticks to make them go away."

Trini and Bobby exchanged looks. This marked the first time they'd heard of creatures in the Bishop neighborhood, closest to downtown.

Weechie got to her feet. "My brother went to the police. They thought he was drunk and told him if he didn't leave, they'd arrest him." Weechie turned to Bobby. "I need to lay down. Would you mind walking me home? I'm scared."

Trini minded. She also wished Bobby would quit looking at Weechie with those big brown eyes of his. She watched them go, teeth clenched, stomach hardening. They looked like Mutt and Jeff walking together. Bobby had to be almost a foot taller. Small consolation.

She had little time to fret. Customers streamed in, full of stories of their own. Perched on a stool at the cash register, she jotted down notes on the pad she used to take inventory. Giant bats with glowing eyes had bashed into the windows of a house in Loma. The Morales family busted up tables to cover the glass to keep them from getting in.

124

Emilio Flores was so shaken up Trini gave him a tequila shot even though it was still morning. The small-built man said something had attacked his goats overnight, their stomachs and throats ripped out, but hadn't seen what did it.

The story Anna Cortez told filled her with a newfound dread.

Anna was a beautiful woman of twenty-five with long, sleek hair. Her parents had sold the family house to the city and left for the San Gabriel Valley, but her husband insisted on staying in Palo Verde. He worked as a night janitor at a hospital near Chinatown, and Anna spent most nights alone. She'd woken to see someone sitting at the foot of her bed, watching her: a fat naked man with a bulbous nose and a lecherous expression. She didn't know how he'd got past their dog, a big, protective mutt, but she'd fought back against his advances and screamed. The dog came running, bit the man on his thick hairy legs, and chased him off. Anna showed Trini the bruises he'd left trying to rip off her nightgown.

When Trini closed up, Bobby had not yet returned. Trini wanted to talk with Lencha, so she went looking for her at Bertita's house.

Bertita was making tortillas while Martin stood at the stove instead of Lencha, stirring a pot of albondigas soup. Bertita tipped her head toward the back door. The two of them made quite a sight, Trini thought, both wearing hats while cooking.

"Lencha's got customers," Bertita said, hands covered with flour.

An understatement, Trini discovered. A long line had formed outside the curandera's shed. It snaked down the alley—people she recognized from around the neighborhoods.

Inside the shed, Lencha was busy filling a glass jar and talking in a soothing tone to Anna Cortez, who looked like she was trying not to cry. The professor sat in a corner, speaking to a balding man with scratches on his face.

Trini settled into the opposite corner, listening as, one by one, customers entered the shed. No one noticed her. They were so wrapped up sharing their tales of what they'd experienced overnight and asking Lencha for protective powders and potions. Residents of all ages. Shoulders curling forward. Rubbing and twisting their hands. Shrill voices, shaking voices, telling their disturbing stories.

Some talked about friends and family who'd had enough and gone to stay with relatives elsewhere in the city.

"Traitors," one old man muttered. Trini winced; not long ago, he could have been talking about her.

When Lencha learned Anna's husband couldn't take a night off from work, she invited the frightened young woman to stay overnight at Bertita's, telling her to bring her dog. Anna broke down crying, relieved she'd not have to spend another night alone, fearing the return of her would-be rapist. Anna arrived at the house in time for dinner.

Bobby appeared as the evening meal was winding up, stepping over Anna's dog Buster, sprawled in the doorway between the kitchen and the hallway. Anna sat in the living room talking to Pete, who had her undivided attention as he told the story of the red-eyed monster, reenacting entire parts.

Salvio sat, listening as everyone told stories about the last twenty-four hours.

"Things are going from bad to worse around here," he said, leaning toward Trini. "This is too much for me. I don't want to be a burden. Feeling useless is a terrible thing when you get to be my age, and that's how I feel. Useless. A pathetic, sick old man. I can't make it on my own. Not with the store, and the house, by myself. I've been thinking about it, Trini. You were right, mija. I should sell up, get the hell out of here for whatever time I have left."

Trini gave her father an incredulous stare as the table got quiet. Her eyes flicked around the table. Nearly everyone looked as stunned as she felt.

Except for Bertita, who was scowling. "Madre mia, Salvio Duran, what's got into you? We said they'd have to drag our bodies out of here," she said, pushing to her feet with a wince. "Or don't you remember?"

Salvio waved a dismissive hand. "That was before. Before all this."

Bertita straightened to her full height. "Bullshit. You want to give up because Trini came back, and now you're afraid. You wanted her help, remember? And here she is. Our own little Anita Oakley. Going out every night and risking her life to save our tired old asses. You owe her more respect, viejo."

Salvio sat back with a huff. He hesitated, then turned to Trini. "I'm sorry, my baby girl. So, so sorry. I should never have made you come." Trini watched as a tear slid down her father's cheek.

It took her a few moments to recover from her shock. Her father never apologized to anyone. "Dad. We can't leave. Our friends, and neighbors, they need us. And we can't let the city people push us around. This is our home. It's paid for, isn't it?"

Salvio nodded. "The market, the house, the places next door. I have the receipts and everything."

Trini blinked back tears. "Okay. Okay, then." She paused and took his chilly hands in hers. "You know why I liked Annie Oakley when I was little? It's because you and mama raised me to be tough and independent. Tough like her and independent like you. When I saw Annie Oakley at the movies, I saw somebody who was like I wanted to be. Someone strong, who never gave up." She blew a kiss to Bertita. "We're staying."

Salvio stared at the floor.

After a few moments, Bobby set down his spoon. "One thing's for sure. We're on our own. The police won't help. I talked to Weechie's brothers and some others down in Bishop about what happened last night. Then I went to see an officer I know. He said we're out of luck. They think we're hysterical up here or lying to get attention."

Trini kissed her father's hands, set them on his lap and jumped to her feet. "Then we're going to need help, because there's not enough of us to fight back. Not even with Ruben and Junie and the guys."

"You need to talk to Henry," Lencha said.

Trini looked at Lencha in surprise. "Henry Loya?" Her boss, she knew, still commanded the respect of the holdouts despite his decision to leave, but she couldn't imagine how the quiet family man could be of any help. At least, the help she was thinking about.

Lencha nodded. "He'll know who to ask, trust me."

Trini and Bobby borrowed Rose Delgado's car to drive to Boyle Heights. They found Henry tinkering with a ham radio in his garage.

"Have a seat," he said, gesturing to some ancient-looking stools.

Bobby wandered over to look at Henry's workbench covered in knobs, wires and circuit boards. "I didn't know you were a ham, Henry."

Henry smiled. "It's just a hobby I picked up." He pointed to a stack of dusty radios. "Some guys I know buy them cheap, then bring them to me to fix, knowing how much I like to tinker. You interested?"

Bobby gave a sheepish grin. "I started a ham radio club in college."

Trini half-listened to this exchange. She was trying to figure out how to proceed. She and Bobby discussed it on the drive from Palo Verde, borrowing Rose's car for their errand. They'd reached no agreement but had prepared themselves for an awkward conversation. Henry was wearing his uniform of gray flannel pants, white shirt, and green smock apron. She couldn't remember him wearing anything else. His hair was thinning on top, and he carried a bit of extra weight around his middle, but he looked as dignified as ever in his black glasses.

"Rose has stopped in a few times," he said, after a long moment. "She's told me what's been going on. I heard from Weechie's father, too. He came by the store this afternoon." He paused, shaking his head. "That poor girl. I'm sure glad she's okay."

"Then, you believe it?" Trini asked in surprise. "The monsters?"

Henry regarded her with solemn eyes. "I do. I've seen some strange things in the ravine myself before all this. Lencha and Bertita have, too." Henry picked up a plug, inspected it, then set it back down on the workbench. "Rose said you were coming," he continued. "Said you needed some help. There's only one person I can think of for a job like this. Ripper Cuevas."

"You called me, boss?" said a voice from the door.

And there stood Ripper, equal parts myth and fact. A former gang member who spent years in and out of jail until Henry had hired him to manage his second store, a decision that surprised many people in Chavez Ravine. Ripper had never married, spending his free time at a boxing gym, giving lessons to juvenile delinquents and helping them go straight. Trini knew about Ripper's past, but it had never fazed her. The only Ripper she'd ever known was honest, hardworking, and minded his own business.

"Hey, Ripper," Trini said, pleased to see him.

He came into the garage, nodding in their direction. "Hey, Trini. Bobby. I thought I heard you in here." Ripper was average height with a sturdy build. He had weathered skin, a thatch of black curls, and a skinny mustache. "I've heard what's going on up there. Sounds pretty bad."

"I went to the police," said Bobby. "We can't count on their help."

Ripper chuckled. "So, what else is new? They don't help Mexicans. They're pretty good at arresting us, though." He grinned, showing straight, white teeth. "From what Henry said, they wouldn't be much help with what we're talking about, anyway. When do you want us up there? Tomorrow? It's too late for tonight."

Trini swallowed, uneasy. "Us?" she asked.

Ripper shot a look at Henry she couldn't quite read. Then he turned back to her and said, "Yeah, me and my buddies. It's time to bust some freak heads. Time to send them back to whatever hell they came from."

Trini felt a tingle run up her spine. A welcome promise wrapped up in a menacing threat.

Bobby was saying something to Henry. "You got some walkie talkies we can borrow? They would come in handy, so we can talk to each other. You know. Coordinate."

"Smart idea, Guerra," Ripper said, coming over and clapping him on the back. "Okay, you bring the radios. I'll bring the boys. We'll meet up tomorrow after the sun goes down."

Chapter 20

Trini spent the day in a state of agitation. Pacing around the market, ringing up groceries, and handing out the wrong change. Imagining the night going terribly, horribly wrong, and Bobby and Ripper dead and bloodied.

By the time dusk arrived, Trini was ready to call the whole thing off. Shooting at monsters when they ran after you was one thing, going after them was another. Ripper didn't know what he was getting into—he hadn't seen the fiends for himself.

When she confided as much to Bobby, he shrugged and said, "It's too late now. They'll be here soon."

Pete and his buddies were so excited about fighting alongside Ripper they arrived hours early, gathering in Bertita's front yard, boasting how many ghouls they would kill. Trini sat on the porch, cleaning her gun for the second time as she kept an eye out for Ripper and his crew.

"Shouldn't they be here already?" she asked Bobby when he brought her a coffee.

Bobby scanned the road, frowning. "It's not even dark yet."

At nine o'clock, there was still no sign of Ripper, and everyone was talking in hushed, worried tones.

Trini paced on the porch, swinging her arms and doing the occasional knee bend. She'd taken to biting her fingernails when she heard a car screeching around the corner. It slammed to a stop in front of the house. Martin was at the wheel. Trini watched, alarmed, as the passenger door flew open and Rose's towering silver bouffant emerged.

"It's Ripper!" she gasped, flapping her hands. "He's not coming. He's been arrested!"

The clock in Duran Market & Liquor had struck noon, and the day already felt hopeless.

Bobby had gone downtown to meet with a lawyer about getting Ripper and his friends out of jail. The police had picked them up at Hollenbeck Park in Boyle Heights, where they'd met with plans to drive to Palo Verde. No one knew why the cops had taken them in.

"I imagine it's because they were hanging around, looking Mexican," Bobby had muttered on his way out.

Trini had never felt so worn out in her life, exhausted by the steady trickle of bad news.

Anna Cortez's husband got off another night shift at the hospital and announced he'd decided to accept the city's lowball offer and sell up. Anna had burst into tears of relief. She wanted nothing more than to leave Chavez Ravine, the place forever ruined by the hairy, naked man everybody now believed to be a monster.

Word quickly spread Ripper and his friends weren't coming to help. For some, it was one blow too many.

"Ai, Trini," said a woman named Espy. "We can't take it anymore. This is no kind of life. There's no point in trying to hang on. For what? The bulldozers are back again in Bishop. They started up again real early. It's terrible what they're doing."

Trini closed up the market and went to look for herself.

She could smell smoke as soon as she hurried past Effie Street. A fire crew was running around, putting out a house set on fire for training exercises. Trini remembered the house. It had been one of her favorites in Bishop, with a pretty porch covered in roses. At the end of the rocky street, a bulldozer bumped along on an enormous pile of rubble as a few onlookers stood by, shoulders slumped in defeat.

The driver of the bulldozer spotted her and gave a loud wolf whistle.

"Go to hell!" she shouted, giving him the finger. The driver gave her the finger in response. She ignored him and turned her back.

"It's the second house they've knocked down this morning," an old man said.

Trini turned to look at him. He had aged since she last saw him, more stooped and wrinkled than before. The same man she used to see in mass at Santo Niño Church in Palo Verde, the elderly gentleman who surprised everyone by dancing up a storm at church festivals.

"Have you sold up?" she asked.

The man sighed. "Not yet, but the time is coming. I don't want to be the only one left. What would happen to me, then? My neighbors look out for me, and they don't want to stay. Not after those damn birds showed up and tried to bite that young lady." His eyes widened in sudden recognition. "Aren't you a friend of that Weechie girl?"

Trini nodded, staring past him at a fire truck rumbling past. There wouldn't be much left of Bishop at this rate.

He tapped her arm to get her attention. "I saw Weechie's father this morning. He's already signed the papers."

"They're leaving?" Trini gasped. "The Mora's?"

Without waiting for an answer, Trini fast marched up the hill to confirm what she already knew: The Mora's had given up. She found Weechie's brothers loading boxes into a truck. She climbed the porch's steep steps and found Weechie inside the kitchen, helping her mother pack.

"I just heard!" she cried. "I can't believe it."

Mrs. Mora straightened up with a groan. "I'm too old for this, Trini. I never thought I'd leave this house. I'm not sure what your mother would say if she'd lived to see it, God bless her soul." Then she gave Trini's cheek a playful pinch. "Weechie would never leave without saying goodbye. She was going to see you as soon as we finished in here."

At this, Weechie burst into tears and threw herself into Trini's arms. Trini returned her embrace with an awkward pat on the back. Her old friend's displays of emotion had always made her feel uncomfortable.

"I'll be closer to you now," Weechie sobbed. "My Dad found a place in Boyle Heights. We can see each other more, right?"

Trini disentangled herself and looked through the window at the wide front porch, where they used to play for hours when they were kids. She couldn't believe Mr. Mora had changed his mind. He'd swore he would never leave. *They'll have to haul me out,"* he'd declared countless times in her hearing.

Pete Chavira appeared from the hallway, staggering under the weight of a heavy box. Blotches of cream still covered parts of his face. He stopped when he caught sight of Trini. "The Mora's had me stay the night," he said, shuffling his feet. "They didn't want those bird things to come back and get me."

Mrs. Mora blessed herself. "Ai, of course not!" she exclaimed. "Not after what La Luz Mala did to your face."

Pete slunk past Trini, who stared after him, lips pursed.

Weechie, wearing a blue housedress with her hair wrapped in a matching headscarf, pulled her into the hallway.

"I hope you don't mind," she said, flushing. "About Pete, and me."

Trini's eyebrows shot up. "Of course not. He's a good guy. Brave." After a moment, noticing Weechie's pained expression, she added. "He's a free man as far as I know."

Weechie lowered her eyes. "You mean not like Bobby. I'm sorry, Trini. I should have told you, but I tried making a move on Bobby. He let me down real nice. Said you and him were going out. Why didn't you tell me?"

"I guess I should have," Trini said, blinking back her surprise.

After promising to visit the Mora's new home once things had settled down, she left, hurrying toward Palo Verde, mind racing. She couldn't think straight with the afternoon sun beating down on her head. The weather had been unpredictable. Warm one day, and cold and windy the next. As unpredictable as Bobby Guerra. What had he meant by telling Weechie they were dating? And it wasn't the first time. He'd said the same thing to Pete but had never gotten around to telling her. Correction. He'd never asked her out. Not in any official way.

By the time she got to the Palo Verde neighborhood, hot and sweaty after her long walk, she'd counted six families packing up to leave.

"We're not staying here one more night!" a lady named Carmen shouted from her porch, broom in hand. "And you shouldn't either, Trini Duran. It's not safe for young women around here no more." Whether Carmen was talking about what happened to Anna Cortez or Weechie Mora, Trini didn't know, and she didn't stop to inquire; she wanted to find Bobby, and fast. It was time they had a talk.

She knocked on Bobby's door, but there was no sign of him. She doubled back to Bertita's and found him sprawled on the couch, staring up at the ceiling. Rose sat perched on a chair next to him, holding a wet towel to his forehead.

Trini's heart lurched in her chest. "What happened?" she gasped. "Is he okay?"

"He's had a rough day," Rose said, using her free hand to point at the tequila bottle in Bobby's hand.

Trini felt a rush of relief. At least he wasn't hurt. She crossed the room and grabbed the bottle, then dropped into a deep easy chair.

"He's not the only one," she said, then took a swig. She made a face. Hard liquor wasn't her favorite, but it would do in a pinch. "What happened, Bobby? Any luck with that lawyer?"

Bobby held up his hands in surrender. "We tried, Trini. We tried," he said, slurring his words. "The police arrested Ripper and his friends for no good reason. Said they were loitering. The lawyer's not sure how long they're going to keep them in there. It doesn't help Ripper and his friends have records. Guilty once, always guilty. That's the way the cops think, especially if you're Mexican."

Rose looked more bitter than Trini had ever seen her. "It's funny, don't you think? Ripper was supposed to rescue us. Ripper! Of all people! It goes to show you how times have changed. I remember him when he was a good-for-nothing punk."

Martin entered the room, carrying a bottle of red wine. He poured Trini a glass and set it next to her on a table. "Here, honey," he said. "This is better for you."

"Thank you, Martin," Trini said, blowing him a kiss. She leaned forward and stuck the tequila bottle back in Bobby's hand. "I saw a bunch of people getting ready to leave. Weechie and her family are going, too."

Bobby closed his eyes. "I heard that. People are throwing in the towel. I tried talking to some of them, but after what they've been through, nothing is going to change their minds."

"Has the professor come back?" Trini asked.

"Not yet," said Rose, accepting a glass of wine from Martin. "Lencha's worried about him. She thinks what he's doing is dangerous, all that poking around into the Tuck man."

Trini sighed, too tired to get up. "Has anyone seen my dad? Is he okay?"

Bobby and Rose exchanged looks. "He's taking a nap, but he's fine," Bobby said, lowering his voice. "Except he's been talking about leaving again. He wanted Rose to drive him downtown to the housing authority. She said she wouldn't do it until he talked with you."

"And I meant it," Rose muttered, staring into her glass.

Trini covered her face with her hands. The day before, she had allowed herself to hope. Hope that Ripper and his friends could save them from the monsters that plagued Chavez Ravine. And now, Ripper was behind bars, and another exodus of residents had begun, one they were helpless to stop.

The city was winning. And so was that damn witch.

Chapter 21

Professor Miller set the book on the counter with a flourish. "It's a lot of gibberish to me," he said.

Trini pushed the cash register drawer closed. The afternoon customers had done more complaining than shopping, so she'd taken in less than eight bucks. She'd spent more time answering questions about Ripper than she had bagging groceries. Not that she had much information to share. Henry Loya had gone to the jail, but an officer sent him away, saying Bruno Cuevas could not receive any visitors.

She picked up the book and studied it—small and heavy. The cover was gray with small black type. She squinted at the title.

"It's not in English," she said, surprised.

The professor gave a quiet laugh. "No. I said Spencer Tuck was a clever man. He wrote the book in Irish, for all the good it's going to do us." He sighed. "I haven't found someone to translate for us, but there are some interesting-looking illustrations in there, but what it all means is anyone's guess. I'm sorry, Trini, I was hoping it would be more helpful."

"Have you showed it to Lencha? What does she say?"

The professor shook his head. "I tried. She won't touch it. To tell you the truth, I think she's afraid of it, and she didn't want me to give it to you, either. If we can please keep this between us."

When the professor had gone, Trini flipped through the pages. There were diagrams with spirals and stars, drawings of circles with letters inside them, and page after page of strange symbols, some in horizontal form, others top to bottom.

Toward the end of the book, she found several drawings of winged creatures and monstrous-looking beasts, but none like she'd seen in Chavez Ravine. She lingered over one picture in particular. It showed a withered tree, symbols carved into its trunk, with spirits rising from twisted roots. She shivered. Some ghosts had skeletal faces and hands like claws. One brandished a scythe.

She closed the book, squeezed her eyes shut for a moment to rid herself of the disturbing images.

Her eyes flew open. There was something familiar about several of the drawings. Something she'd seen on one of her walks across the open hills of La Loma. She'd come across an old well. There were several around Chavez Ravine, this one notable for the graffiti covering it, but not the usual dirty pictures and initials. There had been other drawings, odd ones, but she hadn't given them much thought.

She needed to look at the well again, make sure she wasn't imagining things. No point bothering Bobby until she did.

She changed into her work boots, strapped on her holster, closed the store and set out. The afternoon had warmed up, with a dry wind blowing over the hills. No one was around. Before the people of Chavez Ravine had received eviction notices, kids would have been everywhere, little boys zooming around on their homemade carritos. But now, few children remained. The place had an abandoned, lonely feeling to it.

Trini spotted the well in the distance, partially hidden by a small group of scraggly trees. She approached it warily, patting her gun for reassurance. The wind whipped her hair around her face.

Her mouth was dry, and her neck and shoulders had tensed up so tight they ached. If something moved out here, she'd shoot the hell out of it.

Her eyes widened as she studied the sides of the well. How had she mistaken all those complicated scribbles for graffiti?

Someone had taken the time to carve strange and complex symbols into the wood—some she recognized from Spencer Tuck's book. They looked fresh, stark against the faded boards.

Bobby had to see them right away.

Trini ran down the hill, the warm wind tearing at her clothes. She stopped by the market and grabbed Tuck's book off the counter. At Bertita's house, she dropped to one knee next to Bobby, who was snoring on the couch, still looking impossibly handsome. She shook him by the shoulders.

He grunted in surprise. "What? What's happening?"

She pulled him to his feet. He gazed at her with unfocused brown eyes, then scraped a hand through his hair and yawned. She groaned in frustration. He was no use to her in this state. She shouted at Bertita to bring a cup of coffee while she shoved him toward the bathroom where she kicked the door closed, ran cold water into the bathtub and began unbuttoning his white shirt. He didn't seem to own any other color, although she had to admit it looked nice against his smooth, brown skin.

Bobby protested, trying to wriggle away, but she pressed down on his foot, hard, with a boot, and began unbuckling his belt.

"I can do it, thank you," he said, slapping at her hands.

He dropped his pants.

Bobby wasn't wearing much besides a smug expression, looking amused by the gasp that escaped her lips. Trini felt her toes curl up as her heart galloped in her chest. She swallowed.

"Get in the tub," she said, looking away. "We've got somewhere to go. I need you sober." She flung open the door, and sidestepped out of the room, face burning.

"Don't you want to help me wash up?" Bobby called, then yelped as his body slipped into the cold water.

Bertita appeared at her side. "He's still borracho," she said, handing Trini a mug of black coffee.

Less than an hour later, Bobby was walking at her side in La Loma, his steps becoming steadier, and his gaze more alert. It had been a long and awkward journey. She'd never been in the same room as a naked man, and she didn't know what to think. Bobby didn't seem at all bothered she'd seen him without clothes. Bertita was right. He was still drunk and not thinking straight, although he appeared to follow along fine when she explained her discovery.

He crouched in front of the old well and squinted at the markings. Trini squatted next to him. Together, they thumbed through the pages of the gray book, glancing up to make comparisons. Bobby dug out a pencil and added check marks next to the symbols in the book matching those on the wooden tank.

After entering about a dozen checks, Bobby exhaled and stood up. "I think you're right," he said, pulling Trini to her feet. "I bet this is where those damn things are coming from. Straight out of this well. I haven't seen water in these things for years." He peered inside the dark hole, then drew back. "It looks deep."

Trini stuffed the book into a pocket with a sigh. "I wish we knew what the book said."

Bobby spent a moment lost in pensive silence. "We know enough. These marks have got to be an invitation for the spooks, like the tree in the book."

Trini pushed her shoulders back. "We need to be sure."

Bobby cocked his head and studied her. "I thought you'd say that. Let me guess. You think we should come out here at night, hide someplace and watch?"

Trini shrugged, even though she knew the answer. "Yeah. I guess that's what I'm saying."

Bobby threw back his head and groaned. "You're going to get us killed one of these days."

Trini knew better than to argue. He was right. She watched a crow fly overhead, black against the clear blue sky.

Bobby's face appeared above her. Then he was kissing her, his hands around her waist pulling her closer, arousing nerve endings she didn't know she had. She felt his fingers glide up and down her arms, releasing a delicious warm sensation that spread throughout her body. When he'd stepped back, she gazed into his brown eyes.

"Well…" she began, then ran out of words.

Bobby cleared his throat, a slow smile building until it became a wide grin. He hooked an elbow through hers and began pulling her down the hill.

"I guess that settles that then," he said, sounding pleased.

By the next morning, they had their answer.

They'd witnessed a steady stream of monsters climbing, jumping, and flying out of the well, beginning at eleven o'clock the night before.

It began with a vaporous white cloud drifting upward from the black mouth of the well and spread, in great languorous swirls, down over the hill. Bobby had brought his binoculars and, from their safe vantage point behind a house on a nearby hill, it had all been clear enough.

Everyone gathered in Bertita's living room as dusk approached, the windows boarded up again, ready for whatever horrible things the night might bring.

Trini wished her father had stayed in bed, where he belonged. Walking down the hall to join them had tired him out. He was wheezing, his skin faded and gray. Bertita appeared from the kitchen, hands dusted with flour. She guided him to an easy chair, leaving handprints on his sweater.

"Can we trap them inside the well?" Pete asked, clenching his fists.

"I don't know," Trini said. Bobby was sitting next to her on the floor, one hand resting on her lower back. The warmth of it seeped through her thin shirt.

The professor leaned forward in his chair. "I do," he said. "I found an Irish translator. There was no time for a complete transcription, so I asked her to give it a quick read, see if there was anything that sounded important that we should know about."

Trini felt Bobby's hand twitch against her back. "And?" she said, more loudly than she intended.

"It's not good news, I'm afraid," Professor Miller began, glancing at Lencha. She bit her lip and looked away. "It sounds like the only way to stop them, to send them back to the spirit world, is a sacrifice." He hesitated. "At least that's how the translator interpreted it. She wasn't one hundred percent positive."

Bertita removed her brimmed cap and whacked it against the wall, releasing a cloud of white flour into the air. "If there's one thing we still got plenty of around here is goats. Those monsters haven't got them all yet. Pete can kill a few and throw them down the well."

"I don't think that's the kind of sacrifice the book is referring to," the professor said slowly.

146

All eyes fixed on Professor Miller.

"You mean a human sacrifice?" asked Salvio. "That's what it takes to get rid of those cucuyes?"

The professor nodded.

Trini watched, alarmed, as her father—stone-faced—gripped the sides of the chair like it was about to take off.

A loud banging on the front door made everyone jump.

Rose shrieked and clutched Martin's sleeve. Pete snatched up Bertita's cane and gripped it like a baseball bat. With the windows boarded up, they couldn't see who, or what, was outside.

Bobby recovered first. "Who's there?" he shouted.

Outside, footsteps thudded onto the porch. It sounded like an army was assembling. It was too early to be the creatures, but Trini imagined the worst anyway: the hideous beasts shown in Tuck's gray book gathering outside to put an end to them once and for all.

"Who do you think it is, cabron?" came the unmistakable voice of Ripper. "Open the door. We're hungry."

Chapter 22

At ten o'clock, they were ready to take on the monsters of Chavez Ravine.

This time, they had a full crew. Pete and his buddies, plus Ripper and his dozen men. Weapons ranged from guns and rifles to machetes and metal chains. One guy carried a club with a spiked ball. It made Trini nervous to see Pete's eyes light up as a man with a pock-marked face whipped it around, showing off in the front yard.

"For God's sake, Pete," she said, pulling him away. "Don't get too close, it'll take your face off." Then she gritted her teeth and stalked off. If he got through the night without landing himself into more trouble, it would be a miracle.

She was passing by Ripper when he stepped in front of her, and they nearly collided. "You want to sit this one out, Trini, now that me and the boys are here?"

Trini lifted her chin. "Are you serious?"

"Nah. No way," Ripper said, swinging his lantern. "Your father made me promise to tell you to stay home. You got your gun all cleaned up and ready, Anita Oakley?"

"Just like you taught me," she said, smiling.

"That's right, I forgot," Ripper replied, sounding surprised. "You must have been around twelve when we first went shooting.

When your mother found out, she practically killed me. Damn, that woman was tough."

She watched, biting her lip, as he walked up the dark road. Ripper had insisted on pairing one of his guys with each of Pete's friends. Weechie's brothers had shown up, too, after hearing rumors a battle was afoot. It had taken little convincing to get them to believe monsters had come to Chavez Ravine. They'd seen the birds with bat wings and teeth attack their sister.

Bobby approached, carrying a walkie talkie. Tony had another. They'd tested several locations to find two that offered places to hide and views of the neighborhoods below. They'd use the walkie talkies to let the teams know what the scouts were seeing. This meant Trini couldn't be with Bobby. Instead, she'd take a position down the hill with Junie, who'd already proved himself by stabbing a boogeyman. Junie admitted he didn't like guns, so he'd brought his own bow and arrow and a homemade quiver that looked like it was made from an old tent.

Trini eyed him, muscles twitching. "You sure you know how to use that thing?"

Junie gave her a sideways look with sleepy, hooded eyes. "Yeah. Archery club in high school, and I used to go bow hunting for deer in the San Gabriel Mountains. Plus, I still have my knife."

"Good," she said.

At quarter to eleven, everyone was in position, spread out over the three neighborhoods. The plan was simple—kill as many creatures as possible between midnight and one, the one hour they were vulnerable to physical harm.

Trini had wanted to kill them as they appeared out of the well, but Ripper had nixed the idea. "Hell no. Who knows what they'll do if they're all together. We got to have them separated. On their own. Then we'll pick them off."

Even Bobby had agreed this made sense. Trini supposed it did, too, but she was still anxious.

Ruben, acting as a scout, ran by Trini and Junie just after eleven o'clock. She could hear him panting as he shot up the hill toward Bobby. His voice drifted down toward them.

"They're here," he announced, breathless with excitement. "They're all out of the well."

Trini heard Bobby relay the information to Tony in La Loma on the walkie talkie. "Ruben has eyeballs on the spooks," he said, his voice barely above a whisper.

"Fine business, Bobby," replied Tony.

Junie was using the binoculars to scan the area below. "Are those your jumpers?" he said after a few minutes.

Trini took a deep breath, squinting into the night. And then she saw them. Pale, thin figures in dark robes walking down the rocky road in the general direction of Bertita's house. She wondered what drew them to the place. The size of the house— much larger than the others? The lights on the front porch? Or had they sensed a curandera lived there? Were evil creatures drawn to a hint of magic?

Trini gave a low whistle as a signal to Bobby, then arched her eyebrows at Junie. "Are you ready?"

Junie rose to his feet. "Let's go get them."

A warm wind swept down from the ridge. Trini flung off her jacket, and Junie did the same. It would be easier to move without the bulk. It didn't feel right running next to Junie instead of Bobby. The change made her unsettled and jumpy, wishing she'd never agreed to leave him behind to operate the radio. Walkie talkies had seemed like a good idea, but now, they felt like a useless complication.

They reached the bottom of the hill, ducking through a gap in a fence that stretched along the length of the road. They passed the backs of long-abandoned yards, a rusted jalopy, a dented icebox on its side.

She'd counted on the jumpers taking this route. As planned, Junie ran ahead and climbed a tree overhanging the street. It wasn't the sturdiest specimen. Trini held her breath, hoping it would hold his weight.

The night amplified every sound. Trini could hear the wind rattling the corrugated metal of a lean-to shed, the squeak of a mailbox as it rocked back and forth on its wooden post, an old tarp flapping on a roof somewhere.

She slipped through a gap in the fence, stepping onto the road, terrified of making a sound that would alert the jumpers. They were between her and Junie. Their pale legs and arms appeared lit from within.

Feeling a strange tingling in her chest, she raised her hand over her head and waved. She hoped Junie could see her in the darkness.

Seconds later, she heard an arrow whiz through the air, striking the figure in the middle of the pack. It collapsed with a high, thin wail. The others lifted their heads like dogs sniffing the air. Trini watched, heart sinking, as one moved closer to the fence and looked up into the tree hiding Junie among its branches.

Another arrow came down, striking the creature in the chest. "Please be dead," she muttered.

There were six left. Trini imagined Junie reloading, then wondered how many arrows he had left. She'd forgotten to ask how many he carried in the makeshift quiver strapped across his chest. The pale boogeymen circled, howling at the tree.

Trini heard a rumble of thunder in the distance. Lightning flashed above Elysian Park.

The creatures were jumping, launching high into the air, inching closer to the tree. Their arms and legs didn't look strong enough to climb, Trini noted, and they didn't hold out their hands in front of them as they jumped. How did they expect to grab hold of Junie like that?

Another flash of lightening lit up the sky. At first, she didn't understand what she was seeing—long and thick bands stretching in the air toward the tree. And then she knew.

Tongues. Tongues were coming out of those hideous, wide-open mouths.

"Junie! Get out of…" The words dried up in her throat.

It was too late. A creature had moved close enough to reach its target. Its long, white tongue shot from its mouth and flicked into the tree. Trini heard a scream and the sound of a branch breaking.

Junie crashed to the ground, bringing the pale figure down on top of him. The others gathered around, stooping, their backs to her. She could hear Junie grunting as he desperately fought back. He screamed. Not from fright, Trini realized with horror, but pain.

Fighting a paralysis of fear and unreality, she rushed forward, hand reaching for her gun.

She fired at the closest figure. It staggered, then toppled forward. She was taking aim when two of the creatures jumped into the air over her head, coming to land behind her, boxing her in. As much as she wanted to save Junie from whatever horrible thing was happening, she had to get out. She turned to face the fence and made straight for it, crashing a shoulder against the wooden boards, hitting it with enough force to split the planks, which allowed her to squeeze through the opening.

When she'd put enough distance behind her, she paused long enough to look over her shoulder. They hadn't bothered to follow her. This left her free to climb on top of a wooden shed close to the tree where Junie shot his arrows. The continued noise of

Junie's agonized screams covered any sounds she made in her desperate scramble to the rickety roof.

With trembling fingers, she aimed and fired at the group, still bent over their prey. One fell to the ground with a tremendous jerk, then lay still.

She heard shouts coming down the road.

Bobby. And, by the sound of it, Pete.

She watched as two pale figures straightened and turned to face the incoming threat. Their long, white tongues retracted into their mouths.

Trini heard herself screaming warnings. "Stay back. Cuidarse. Be careful." Bobby and Pete ignored her pleas and kept coming.

Planting her feet wide on the roof of the shed, she pointed the gun with a sudden feeling of calm and pulled the trigger. One went down with a yowl like an injured animal. She fired a second shot to make sure it would stay down. Pete jumped over the prone figure and, with a roar, threw a machete at the creature bent over Junie. It toppled sideways.

Trini flung herself off the roof of the shed and onto the road and sprinted toward Bobby as the long, white tongue of the last jumper whipped around his neck.

Bobby's eyes bulged. Loosening his grip on the baton, it fell to the ground. He used both hands to beat at the tongue, face grimacing with the effort.

Trini stepped forward and shoved her gun into the side of the Cucuy's head, its profile flat and featureless, and fired. The tongue fell from Bobby's neck, and the creature crumpled to the ground. She kicked it with her boot. Bobby flashed a light on it. Its tongue hung out of its head, something black and sharp quivering at the end.

She felt herself swaying on her feet. Bobby pulled her close, so her head rested on his shoulder.

"Are you okay?" he asked, tugging a braid. When she nodded, he led her to where Junie lay on the ground, still writhing, his face swollen and raw looking.

"Those tongues had stingers," she said. "We need to get him to Lencha." She turned to Bobby. "You have to go! Call Tony on the radio to send some help." There was only one bullet left. With shaking hands, she reloaded and shoved the gun into Bobby's hand.

For a moment, she thought Bobby would argue. Instead, he grabbed Pete by the shoulders and gave him a shake. "Watch out for Trini while I'm gone."

Pete strode to the jumper and yanked his machete from its dead body. Trini sat on the ground and cradled Junie's head on her lap, hoping someone would come soon. Pete kept watch and cursed while she tried to say a prayer, but she couldn't seem to remember the words.

"You're going to be fine, Junie. Fine," she said through her tears.

Around them, the bodies of the fiends began to twitch. For one terrible moment, Trini thought they were coming back to life. Instead, they liquefied until only foul-smelling, black puddles remained.

Trini could hear the screams of men echoing through the canyons.

At one-thirty in the morning, everyone regrouped.

They sat huddled in an empty house in Loma, listening to Ripper. The monsters had swarmed them—flying birds with teeth; a man with horns and wings of a buzzard; shadow creatures with glowing red eyes with the power to hypnotize; hairless animals with thick, wrinkled skin with four legs and human-like hands. Dog-Face Bride had lunged at Ripper, going for his throat, but Ruben had come along and speared it dead. Two of Ripper's men didn't make it.

Then, it was Trini's turn. She told the exhausted survivors about the jumping demons with tongues, Pete's machete, and Junie and his arrows. But Junie hadn't survived either.

Tony and Ruben had carried Junie's body to Bertita's house, crying openly as they went. Ripper's men sat in stunned silence. The monsters had forced them to retreat, and no one had suggested they go back for another round.

"Now what?" Trini asked.

Ripper shrugged. "I don't know." He lit a cigarette. "But we've got a problem. It's not like an army. A human army. That witch guy can keep sending more, right?"

Trini felt Bobby's hand squeeze her knee. She leaned her head on his shoulder and closed her eyes for a moment. Ripper was right. She hadn't thought things through. Spencer Tuck had endless resources of evil. A bottomless well full.

Fighting back against spirits meant death surrounded them. Junie was dead, along with two other men. And she was to blame.

Tony and Ruben appeared in the doorway. "Your father's gone, Trini," Ruben gasped.

Trini shot to her feet. "What do you mean, gone? Is he…" She couldn't bring herself to say the word. Dead.

Ruben shook his head. "No! He's not at the house and they can't find him."

Trini fingered the pendant of El Santa Niño her father had given her. "But he's had a heart attack! He can barely walk."

Tony tugged his beanie lower on his forehead and said, "We can't find the professor either, and somebody took my motorcycle. Lencha thinks the professor borrowed it. The ladies are going crazy."

Trini gasped. "They must be together. Where the hell would they have gone?"

Tony cleared his throat. "Lencha thinks they went to the well."

There was a moment of stunned silence.

Then everyone was talking at once, grabbing weapons, making for the door. Trini's legs were shaking so badly she had a hard time walking straight, but it didn't matter. Bobby pulled her along in their wake. She had thoughts so wild they caused her to stumble. Like the professor had rushed her father to the French Hospital because he'd had another heart attack, this one possibly fatal. Or her father had insisted on following her because he was desperate with worry and they were dead somewhere, victims of the monsters.

As they made their way to the well, shots rang out several times. She heard men and things struggling in the dark; loud and terrible animal noises, then grunts and squeals. But every time she stopped to look around, adrenalin shooting through her veins, Bobby urged her forward.

"They're okay," he said.

Finally, she was staring up at the hill.

Her father stood to the right of the well, swaying, the professor propping him up.

Trini couldn't seem to make her feet move. Then her father turned. She shouted his name—Ripper and his men watching her, but remaining where they stood, keeping a respectful distance.

She wondered why no one was rushing up the hill. To bring them back down. And then she understood.

"Dad!" she screamed. "Don't! You can't!"

Salvio Duran held up a hand and waved. It reminded Trini of newsreels she'd seen at the movies, showing people waving goodbye from a ship before it left port.

"I'm a dead man," he shouted. "I don't have much time left, but I can do this one thing. Watch out for these people. God knows they have a right to stay in their homes. It's time for me to be with your mother. I will always love you, hija."

Trini watched as her father lifted himself to a sitting position on the thin edge of the well, teetering precariously. He swung his legs around until he was facing away from her, leaned forward and disappeared.

Chapter 23

Trini's father came to her in her dreams. Begging her not to leave Chavez Ravine. Then he was standing by the well. Hands held her back as she watched him wave and then, in a moment, gone forever.

One week after her father's death, she woke crying. Bobby rolled to his side to look at her. After he'd wiped the tears from her eyes and brushed the damp hair from her forehead, he held her close for a few moments before releasing her with a sigh.

"You want some coffee?" he asked.

She nodded, suddenly feeling shy. She still wasn't used to seeing Bobby in her bed. Bobby, dressed in crisp white shirts and flannel pants, was handsome in a respectable way. Naked, with his sculpted chest and muscular legs, he was beautiful in a way that made her think of sex. Thoughts and actions she was sure were disrespectful for a grieving daughter and sinful to boot. She'd never come close to having sex with another man. Good Catholic girls didn't, but it hadn't felt wrong with Bobby. Despite everything she'd ever heard about the evils of unmarried girls having relations before marriage, it wasn't the shameful act she'd imagined. And it made her feel alive.

They were staying in her father's house. At her request, Bobby had moved his things into her place. There was no point sneaking around. Besides, no one cared what anyone else was doing these days.

Secrets kept for years had fallen away.

Rose moved in with Martin in Loma. His house had a wide porch and a pretty rose garden she looked forward to working in. Lencha and Professor Miller moved into Lencha's tiny house at the bottom of Brooks Avenue in Loma and were fixing it up, although Lencha still saw Bertita daily. Pete's family sold their house to the city and moved to El Monte, so Pete rented a room from Bertita. He'd taken a liking to the tough old lady and didn't want her living alone. Bertita pretended not to notice when Weechie stayed overnight.

Trini dressed for the day in a skirt and blouse, fixing her hair in two loose braids out of habit. Her gun sat on the nightstand, although she had no reason to use it since the monsters hadn't returned after that terrible night when her father threw himself into the well as a sacrifice. Bobby thought it also had something to do with Spencer Tuck losing the election and his seat on the city council.

In a newspaper interview, Tuck expressed bitterness at his defeat and said he planned to move back to Ireland. Bobby concluded he'd lost all interest in Chavez Ravine, so there was no use summoning monsters to scare off the holdouts. There was still no word on what the city meant to do about the people still resisting eviction.

Bobby reappeared, still naked, holding two mugs. Trini sipped the coffee—milk and sugar, exactly how she liked it—and kept her eyes fixed on his.

"I'm going to tell Henry today I'm not coming back to work," she announced.

"You're keeping the market?" he asked, breaking into a smile.

160

She nodded. "I am. And the house and apartment, too. I'm staying. Until they force us out. The people need a market closer than town."

Neither spoke for a moment. Bobby set down his cup, grabbed a robe, and put it on. "That means we can stay together," he said, his voice tinged with hope. "If you'll let me," he added. "You're the property owner. What about your brother? What does he say about all this?"

Trini shrugged. "Beto? I called him from Martin's yesterday. He said it's up to me, as long as he doesn't have to do anything." She paused long enough to roll her eyes. "And gets half of everything when we sell. That's all Beto cares about. Hopefully, I'll make enough money to go to college full time." She hesitated. "Are you sure you want to stay? You don't have to, because of…" Her voice drifted off as her eyes wandered across the unmade bed.

A mischievous smile played around his lips. "Especially because of…" he said, tipping his head toward the bed. Then, he took the mug from her hand, set it down next to her gun, and pulled her close. "My mom invited us for dinner tonight," he said, his lips brushing hers.

Trini swallowed. "She knows about me?"

Bobby grinned. "Of course she does. I tell my mother everything." Seeing her expression, he added, "Okay, not *everything*. She and my aunt want to meet you."

"Okay," she said, plucking at the threads of the chenille spread. "What if she doesn't like me?"

Bobby mulled this over. "Well, she doesn't like anyone who makes her son unhappy. Which means you have to say yes."

"Yes, to what?" asked Trini, eyes widening.

"To me," he said, his voice thick with emotion. "To getting married. Because I love you. I know it's soon, but after everything we've been through together, why wait? What do you say?"

Trini put her arms around his neck, a tear sliding down her cheek. "My dad liked you. It would have made him happy to see us together. And yes. Of course, the answer is yes."

They ate breakfast, then Bobby went into town for a union meeting, and Trini opened the market for the first time since her father died. People trickled in and gave their condolences. Some wanted to attend the funeral. Rose had helped with the arrangements for the services at La Placita Church on Main Street downtown.

They'd not said anything to Father Peralta about monsters or a sacrifice. He believed Salvio Duran had died from a tragic fall. Ripper and two of his guys had recovered her father's broken body from the well. They had seen nothing strange when they'd gone down there, but they described a terrible cold seeping from cracks in the ground, chilling their bones and filling them with a dread that lingered for days.

In between customers, Trini began work on a large sign. She used stiff white paper and bright red paint she found in the storeroom. Weechie stopped by during lunch and helped her hang it up in the plate-glass window of the market.

Then they went outside in the warm fall sunshine and surveyed the results.

Weechie tilted her head, hands on her hips, and said, "I like it. Did Bobby think of the wording?" Trini experienced a familiar flash of irritation. Weechie had a special gift for saying things that got on her nerves.

"No," she said. "I thought of it all by myself."

Trini turned back to the sign and gave it her full attention. Bobby, she thought, would be pleased.

It read, "IT'S NOT TOO LATE TO SAVE CHAVEZ RAVINE."

Chapter 24

On a crisp November morning, Trini buried her father at Evergreen Cemetery in Boyle Heights in a plot he'd paid for in cash six months before his death. He'd wanted to ensure he had a place next to her mother.

Downtown loomed in the distance. The mourners stood sheltered from the brilliant sunshine under the shade of an enormous willow tree.

The large turnout for the graveside service had not surprised Trini. Salvio Duran had been born in Palo Verde, and in his many years running one of the few grocery stores in the three neighborhoods above the hills of Los Angeles, he'd encountered just about everyone who'd called it home. Those who didn't know him had come out of respect for her mother, whose family first arrived from Mexico in the 1920s. The few surviving aunts and uncles Trini still had couldn't make it. They'd moved to Arizona when she was a kid and hardly knew them.

Trini half-listened to the words of Father Peralta. A family crypt beyond the priest distracted her from the service. The stone building tilted, and its decorative iron gates had come off its hinges. For one dark, horrible moment, she imagined Dog-Face Bride emerging from its shadowy interior. She squeezed her eyes shut.

After Father Peralta had committed her father's body to the earth, everyone lined up to tell her what a wonderful man her father had been.

She asked Bobby if they could take a walk before heading back to Chavez Ravine for the reception at Bertita's house.

"Sure," he said, sounding surprised. He stared down at Salvio Duran's memorial card with El Santo Niño de Atocha on the front. "I have an idea. There's something you should see."

"Here?" she asked, surprised. She hoped it wasn't one of the crypts that surrounded them.

Bobby tucked her hand under his arm and led her to the eastern corner of the cemetery. She wished she'd worn more comfortable shoes. Walking across the crabgrass in heels was making her ankles ache, and she'd lost her shoe more than once by stepping into an in-ground flower vase, each time eliciting a gasp. She guessed it would take more time before her nerves recovered from the dark happenings at Chavez Ravine.

"Well, one thing's for sure. The supernatural is real," Bobby said. Something she'd rather forget, but there was little chance of that. Lingering fear had combined with sharp pangs of grief over her father.

After the long wake the night before, she was too tired and numb to talk. Bobby was content to walk by her side, silent but comforting. Occasionally, they stopped to look at small oval photos on the stones. A Japanese American couple, both distinguished with silver hair and glasses. A sweet-faced African American boy in a hat, ten years old.

Bobby eventually stopped in front of a large memorial stone with a statue of a roaring lion on top.

She read the engraving: "Pacific Coast Showmen's Rest Association. Organized 1922."

"What is this?" she asked, looking around at the grave markers dotting the dry lawn. There were no trees in this part of the cemetery.

Bobby put an arm around her shoulder. "I remember you told me you liked reading about Annie Oakley and the circus, and I remembered this. Carnival workers are buried here. The acrobats and the clowns. People from the sideshows. Hundreds of them. The association thought they needed a resting place after all those years on the road."

The tears were coming now: for her father, for Junie, for Ripper's friends who had given their lives to banish the monsters terrorizing Chavez Ravine. For Hal, the gringo bachelor killed in the little shack he'd called home. And for all the people buried under the ground beneath their feet whose names she would never know.

She leaned her head on Bobby's shoulder. "Thank you," she whispered. "Thank you for showing me this."

The reception at Bertita's house started tamely enough. The holdouts of Chavez Ravine cycled through, sharing their memories of Salvio Duran. Trini's nephews ignored Trini in favor of Bobby, who taught them to play a new card game. Then they ditched Bobby for Henry Loya's boys when her former boss and wife walked in the door.

Soon, it sounded like old times in Chavez Ravine, with children yelling and playing in the street. There was enough food to feed an army of mourners: tamales, menudo, pozole, rice, beans.

Trini went into the kitchen and wrapped her arms around Bertita's angular frame. The old woman smelled of cigar smoke and Coty's face powder. "You've been so good to me. Thank you."

Bertita kissed her forehead, then swatted her behind. "Ai. It's nothing. Your father was always good to us. All those years, but especially at the end..." The old woman paused as tears welled up. "And, besides, Weechie helped me," she said, recovering. "She's not bad in the kitchen. And, by the sound of it, she's not bad in the bedroom either." Then she tipped her head toward Pete and wriggled her eyebrows suggestively.

Trini laughed. She had a whole new appreciation of Bertita after everything they'd been through together. In fact, that summed up how she felt about everyone: Rose, Martin, Pete, and his friends, and Lencha. Her thoughts on Weechie had changed little. Weechie was sitting on Pete's lap, bragging about her new job as a seamstress to a fashion designer.

As the evening wore on, a small band arrived. Trini wasn't sure who asked them to come. After an hour had gone by, she told the bass player to quit with the sad music and play something everyone could dance to. Her mother would have been scandalized but knew her dad would have understood. People were tired of being sad and afraid. In one week, they'd buried her father, Junie and two of Ripper's crew.

They'd survived and deserved to have some fun.

Soon, Rose was spinning around in Martin's arms in the living room. Trini didn't know the two could dance so well. The black lace veil pinned to the top of her silver bouffant didn't fall off during their exertions. Weechie, of course, had to show off her dance skills, although Pete had two left feet and had a hell of a time keeping up.

Trini escaped to the front porch with a glass of red wine.

Lencha and the professor soon joined her.

"If this had been last week, we would have been boarding up the house by now." Trini held up an unsteady hand. She'd had a few glasses of wine and was feeling a bit wobbly. "Don't worry, professor. I'm not mad at you. Not anymore. I understand why you did what you did, helping my father."

Trini watched the professor exhale. "I was hoping you'd forgive me, Trini. Not that I deserve it. I'm still not sure I made the right choice in taking him to the well. It's something I'll have to live with the rest of my life."

"But he asked you," Lencha said. "When a dying man asks a favor, it's not right to say no."

Trini's eyes pooled with tears. "I talked to Dr. Eng. I wish they would have told me the truth. I would have come back sooner." She sniffed. "He said my dad wouldn't have made it another six months, not with his heart in that condition."

Lencha and the professor exchanged anxious looks.

"What?" Trini asked, crossing and uncrossing her legs. "What is it?"

"There's something we haven't told you," said Lencha, folding her hands in her lap. She was wearing a simple black dress. Trini thought she looked beautiful.

The professor cleared his throat. "When I was looking into Spencer Tuck, I talked to many people. One of them was also a practitioner of witchcraft, focused on positive spells and doing good. After your father died, I visited the man and told him the whole story. He was quite shocked. He has no experience with this sort of thing, but he wanted to help us. To make sure we've put an end to it. Properly."

An icy jolt of fear shot up Trini's spine. "What do you mean, properly? My dad sacrificed himself. Are you saying that wasn't enough?"

Professor Miller shook his head. "No, apparently not. He believes Tuck opened a portal between our world and the spirit world. Your father sacrificing his life closed it, but Tuck is an angry man. Angry at the people here for defying the eviction orders and keeping him from getting his way. It's possible that he could unleash those demons again."

Trini gasped. "Then what are we going to do? We can't have those monsters coming back!" She looked around wildly. "Where's Bobby? He needs to know, too."

Lencha leaned forward and took her hand. "We've already told him, mija. He's getting ready. Ripper and Pete are coming, too."

Trini lifted her head at the sound of the front gate creaking open. Bobby, dressed in dungarees and an old shirt, was holding a shovel in one hand and her work boots in the other. Ripper and Pete, too, had changed out of their funeral clothes. Each carried brown haversacks and a shovel. All wore solemn yet determined expressions. Trini tugged on the boots, and together, the group made their way to La Loma and climbed the hill to the well. The professor followed on the motorcycle with Lencha.

The setting sun put on a glorious show for the little procession—a purple sky streaked with orange and yellow clouds. Trini squinted at the strange symbols still etched on the side of the well.

"What are we doing?" she asked.

Lencha took a deep breath before replying. "The witch John talked to says my magic is strong enough to do this." She gave a self-conscious shrug. "I told him I was a healer and not a bruja, but he didn't believe me."

Trini was still mystified but remained silent as Ripper handed around wire brushes and paint scrapers. Kneeling, the men set to work scrubbing the carvings of the magical symbols. When they finished, Ripper and Pete used blow torches to burn off the remnants. Wielding sledgehammers, they knocked down the sides of the well until all that remained was a large hole in the ground.

Trini turned her back for this part. She couldn't bear to look at the black cavity where her father had died.

Pete dragged the busted planks several yards away and buried them.

"It's too deep to fill with dirt and rocks," Bobby said, staring into the pit.

Ripper pointed to a piece of sturdy plywood lying on the ground nearby. "We dropped it off earlier," he said.

Pete placed the plywood on top of the hole, then hammered it into place. Bobby stepped forward and helped shovel dirt until a mound had formed.

"After a while, no one will know a well was ever here," Bobby said.

The men packed up their tools. Trini watched as Lencha stepped forward, placed a dish towel on the ground in front of the heap of dirt, and knelt. She removed a pouch the size of a baseball from the pocket of her black dress and lifted it high into the air. The professor lit the pouch with a match. Trini saw Ripper make the sign of the cross. Then Pete and Bobby did, too. She clutched the El Santa Niño medallion her father had given her and said a short prayer.

A bitter fragrance filled the air. The smoke trailed in black wisps into the sky above La Loma.

Sitting again on Bertita's porch, drinking wine, Trini, feeling more than a little drunk, said, "Do you think it worked, Lencha? What you did at the well?"

Lencha was silent for a long time. "Remember when I told you I wasn't a witch? Just a healer?"

Trini nodded.

"When I was at the well, I felt something different. Like I had magic. Real and powerful magic." Lencha paused and gave a self-satisfied smile. "I did something. Something to give us a little insurance policy."

The curandera's smile faded, and a shadow came over her face. "I made a special spell. If all of us go, and we have no ancestors in this place, then the monsters will come back in one hundred years." Her eyes narrowed. "If we can't live here, the people of Loma, Palo Verde and Bishop, then no one else is going to have it, either."

Seeing Trini's shocked expression, Lencha's smile returned. "Don't worry, mija. All of us will be long gone by then."

Trini sighed. It had been a long day, and she'd had enough of that kind of talk. She didn't think she'd ever see Lencha in quite the same way.

She went inside and thanked Bertita, Rose and Weechie for the reception, said the rest of her goodbyes, then hauled Bobby off the couch.

Hands around each other's waists, they walked up the road to her house. The house where she'd been born. The house she wasn't leaving until they carried her out.

Afterword

The Elysian Park Heights public housing project planned for Chavez Ravine never happened. The political winds of the 1950s swept it away. Construction of the massive project once touted for the public good found itself associated with socialism and "un-American spending." Those labels doomed it. Some complicated wrangling followed, resulting in the cancellation of the plan, and the land being earmarked for a future public purpose.

Eventually, the neighborhoods of Palo Verde, La Loma and Bishop would become ghost towns, with fewer than two dozen families still living in Chavez Ravine, holding out against eviction.

In 1958, Los Angeles voters approved a proposition in favor of a contract for the land between the Dodgers and the City of Los Angeles.

In May 1959, sheriff's deputies forced out the last of the residents and four months later, in September, construction began on Dodger Stadium.

Glossary

Note: The definitions provided are those used in the context of this story.

Borracho: drunk
Bruja: witch
Cabron: dumbass
Carritos: little cart; wagon (made for children)
Cojones: testicles
Con cuidado: carefully
Cucuy: boogeyman
Cuidate: take care of yourself
Curandera: healer; medicine woman
Diablo: devil
Elote: Mexican sweet bread with a texture resembling a cookie
Gringos: American
Jefe: boss
Hija: daughter
Los viejitos: The old men (the old people)
Madre mia: Oh Dear/Oh God
Madre mia de Dios: my mother of God
Mentira: lie
Mija: my daughter (a colloquial contraction)

Nalgas: buttocks
Pendejo: idiot/fool
Pan dulce: Mexican sweet bread
Pinche: strong swear word meaning "shitty," among other things
Semita: Mexican sweet bread made from wheat
Si: yes
Vaya con Dios: go with God
Viejo: old man
Viejitos: old men

Author's Note

When I was growing up, my mother and the rest of her family would often reminisce about their old neighborhood of Palo Verde, and the friends they had in La Loma and Bishop. Sometimes, later in life, they referred to it as Chavez Ravine.

The story of the fight to save the villages from destruction through eminent domain evictions is filled with brave people challenging injustice. Out of respect for their memories, I have not included them in this story. To get one small detail wrong would be to do them a great disservice.

While the battle over Chavez Ravine depicted in the story generally follows the sad trajectory that happened in real life, it fictionalizes the politicians, as it does the contentious public meeting in which the character Bobby Guerra speaks.

If you're interested in learning more about the history of the area, I've compiled a list of recommended reads on my website, debracastaneda.com. There, you'll also find an artistic illustration of the main character, Trini Duran, based on my mother at age twenty-two.

Thank you for choosing to read this story. For that, I'm extremely grateful! As an independent author, reviews can make all the difference in getting the word out. If you enjoyed *The Monsters of Chavez Ravine*, I hope you consider rating it and leaving a review on Amazon and/or Goodreads.

About the Author

Debra Castaneda's recent works include *The Box in The Cuts*, a supernatural mystery for young adults, and a horror novelette, *The Root Witch: An Urban Legend Caught on Tape*. She's currently at work on Book 2 in the Samantha Reyes mystery series, *The Break in The Cuts*.

After a career as a journalist in radio and TV, she now devotes her time to writing fiction. She lives with her husband in Capitola, California.

Made in the USA
Las Vegas, NV
16 August 2021

28251017R00109